I0659190

PHOENIX'S ETERNAL FLAME

RAVEN HUSH

First Edition

Published by Little Quail Press

Ebook ISBN 978-1-922448-58-3

Paperback ISBN 978-1-923471-05-4

BLURB

Existing for thousands of years can be boring...until an unlikely scientist tries to pop my lava cherry.

Metaphorically speaking, of course. That cherry got popped a while back and I've been stuck on a tiny island with hardly anyone to talk to since.

Which is why Sinclair Kincaid is so fascinating. Dorky, cute, and full of good intentions, he's in a place he shouldn't be at the right time because this lava girl wants to get her magma off this rock...and he's my ticket across the ocean.

He just doesn't know it yet. But if I heat things up for us, I'm scared he might take more than my body with him...he might just get my heart, too.

For my little pyro.

PROLOGUE

The first flick of flames caressed my ankles, winding around my calf. They warmed my skin with a gentle kiss as I twisted and writhed beneath their surprisingly gentle touch.

Intimate, like a lover.

And inside, I burned.

I held my legs apart as the heat of me dripped onto the engulfing mass that sizzled with the scent of long held desire.

Long, because it took an eon for me to find someone suitable as a mate. But none of them survived my full heat. And I couldn't control it.

Eyes glowed at me over the embers I stood on, barefoot, dancing, and twirling, my arms raising and falling. Eyes filled with lust, as yet unstated. Two legendary creatures ready to merge in the most primal way.

Soon.

But still, I danced. My body undulated, my skin ablaze beneath the fire, its fingers winding along my body and into my hair, lifting it from my head.

Aglow. Aflame.

Nothing compared to this. Nothing, not even the touch of the warrior opposite me who fought his way to my island and wrestled the elements of my volcano just to be here.

He either wouldn't survive the night, or he would return to his people and brag of his night with the fire girl he tamed.

That last part was never true.

None of them ever stayed. And so, the act itself meant nothing to me, and I took my time and danced to the flames that, like me, would live forever. Immortality in the heart of the fire pit burning like an eternal flame.

Ever alone.

CHAPTER ONE

BLAZE

I sat on the top of my hill, running my fingers across my salamander's back. "They never learn, do they?"

Nahi glowed a pretty blue, and gave a little shiver as I played with his tail. The tiny creature stared at the boat that drifted across the horizon, the encroaching craft headed toward my island.

An unwelcome boat, carrying unwelcome visitors.

It didn't matter what they wanted or what form humanity took, but always they were the same. Taking my rocks, treading over the sacred heart of this place without reverence. In ancient times, I survived by fear alone–and always remained alone, of course–because fear and monsters only had a lonely existence if they wanted to exist for longer than a single moon. And so in a bid to live my immortal life, I chose to be alone. And remained a monster.

Today, I refused to be no less.

A gentle pressure of teensy feet brought me back to my island, and out of my head. My salamander, squishy and tiny, always retained the warmth of my volcano. His body glowed a happy orange as he nestled against my thigh, his sky-blue flames melding into a sunset colored visited on my leg.

I tucked to my knees beneath me, letting my hair with its flames drape along my back. They had their own personality, flicking and dancing independent of my control. Think Medusa, but with flames instead of snakes. Less instant death and more eternal torture unless I put them out myself.

If that made me a monster, then so be it.

And I let them believe that, the people who came to my island. The ones that claimed they owned it, or dropped the bombs at its testing grounds. The people who adored me for so long forgot they knew anything about me other than my name, if that. I drifted into the realm of legend and where forgotten memories lay. I became the shadow not to be talked about. Because if you saw my light, death followed fast after.

The people with their endless line of warriors who wanted to claim my fire for themselves. Thousands of years, thousands of warriors. And none of them shared even a mortal life with me, not a flicker of passion or love. My island simply was a house for the trapped fire girl and a place to shove their cold, heartless rods into my molten core.

Perhaps that was poetic. Who knew? The world turned on and left me behind, though my island reclaimed. The untouched place for scientists and soldiers to alternate possession of, depending on their mood, it seemed, or what they needed most. I managed to steal one of the strange devices the last group of scientists left on my island. Hiding in the shadowy cracks I found that a geeky science man had a penchant for some very steamy Viking warriors. Vikings were new to me, but then my world was limited to a single volcano in the middle of the Pacific Ocean.

But the device didn't last forever, and its screen went blank before I could read through all the delicious romances within its metal clutches.

Sunlight reflected on the boat that drifted across the horizon. I scooped up my salamander, placing the little lizard on my shoulder where he curled around my neck like a torc.

Another Viking word I liked. Perhaps I could find some precious metals within the volcano, some obsidian, or other volcanic glass and fashion jewelry for myself.

What else does a girl do when she has eons to live and no other form of entertainment other than spontaneously combusting every now and then?

"They'll come soon." I pensively watched the boat that stilled.

The research vessel was far too large to pull in close to my shallow shores with its small lagoon and brutal reef beyond. Many a new ship, so much larger than my warrior's canoes, tried to enter my bay ,only to flounder. Then I would sit within my cave, peering out and hoping no one saw me while I laughed at their efforts, praying they would stay for my pleasure, and never return for my safety.

Maybe my sanity.

Every now, I flowed between the cracks of the island in my flame form, all the way to the seashore, watching the waves lap softly against the sandy shores. I'd sit there, creating a trail of fragile, twisted glass in tortured patterns there amongst the tiny grains that measured the absence of time and history between us all at once.

Never had I been any closer to the water, not anymore. Only once, and that was a long, long time ago. Because I knew what would happen. First, I'd be fascinated by the color, the motion so similar to my own flames, the way the waves scooped and flicked at the sand like it, too, consumed. I'd want to touch it. And like a child, I'd reach out a finger waiting, sun warming the water as it kissed my skin.

But in reality, that dream could never eventuate. The water was never warm, and only icy torture filled my veins until I reared back, a screaming mass from the ocean's mirror-like surface. My skin faded to the pale blue of Nahi's flames, and I'd freeze into place, a flame-shaped statue left on the shore for the next visitors to find.

All from a simple touch of the water that was life to everything else, and death to me. Then I scuttled back to my volcano, sinking into the blessed warmth and safety of my lava bath, my eyes scrunched shut as I tried to cry. Tears of pure anguish that never came. Then, with the pain that came after, I lay beneath the surface, flickering and helpless, relegated to the Island as my home and my cage.

Because I tried to escape. Or feel.. Because I chose to take control of my own destiny.

Because of who I am.

My body shuddered in a full body effort that rocked me where I stood. The boat was much closer now. I slapped my palms to the steaming rocks, knowing I caused their changed state in my moment of memory.

One the water, a bright orange tender departed from the boat–ship's, it looked much larger now–side, headed towards me.

I sighed, soaking in the sun's rays as best I could in my short time remaining on the surface as the little boat scooted closer across the waves. Finally, I knew I couldn't stay out, not unless I wanted my trip off the island to be in a test tube, sliced and poked and prodded by the scientists who studied my rocks, or soldiers who disarmed the remaining bombs littering my rocks.

But always their eyes flickered to the old volcano, searching, searching.

For me.

A long sigh left me. "It's time to go inside."

Nahi chattered in his squeaky voice softly and burst into flame, leaving me with the necklace of burning lizard.

I smiled. Maybe it was time to hunt for some of that metal.

Maybe I could come back and talk to the scientists, if they didn't have a military cohort as their escort.

Or maybe...I could liberate some of those snazzy little power banks that ran on solar power. I learnt lots from my scientists, though they never saw me. I made sure they didn't. Because as much as I was alone, letting them know I was here was a greater risk. I knew this type, had seen them before. The ones who like to discover everything by taking it away from its home and cutting it into many pieces and storing them in tiny jars with lids on.

I imagined slips of my hair cut off and flaming away from me, only to be snuffed out when they put the lid on and extinguished all the air that I enjoyed heating and playing with. Flames were always playful, even when they were hungry, but without anything to consume, in a cage of whatever making, I would suffocate. Slowly.

Maybe they do that to me, too. Extinguish what I needed to exist, that kept me going. Until all that remained was hardened, black shell, unmoving until I was returned to my volcano and my lava bath inside.

The power that heat gave me rocketed through my core, emanating from the inside out. My hair lifted into the air around me like a halo of pure sunlight.

But I was so much more dangerous than the sun.

The scientists pulled their boat onto the beach, escorted as always by a man with a gun. Weapons might change over the eons, but people didn't. His fear carried to me on the wind like a palpable thing.

That wasn't a fight I could win today, or any other.

I pressed a hand to Nahi, carrying my companion back up the hill and slipped through the crevice just large enough for one person and into my caves, trailing my fingers along the walls. Here, they were only warm, but the deeper into my cave I tread, the warmer each cavern became.

A few of the surface caves were cool enough that the hard rock between the magma and the surface created a space where humans could settle there safely. My volcano hadn't erupted in eons, and it hadn't rumbled enough recently to indicate it would again any time soon. Those caves were full of draw-ings along the walls and roof of my life and those who came to visit. Each warrior added a little gift until I had my very own shrine, place of worship for the living already dead, and passed from history.

I never let the scientists or the new style warriors find that place.

Standing at the edge of one of the surface caves, I watched our visitors mill about, some with purpose, others wandering and studying the ground like it held the answers to whatever questions they sought.

Spoilers: they didn't.

"I want to read those books," I whispered from the shadows, craning for a glimpse of their equipment as they unpacked.

Nahi rubbed against my cheek. His flames licked my lips, and I bumped my nose at him when he reached up with a tiny foot. "You're too cute. And a nice distraction. But I still want to read those books."

I only made it through a dozen or so before the screen blacked on me. But now was not the time to find what I needed. I'd have to wait until darkness, and so I slipped into mine, letting the underside of the island swallow me where warmth and time melded, and I forgot about my worries, letting the heat sink heart deep as I had for an age, or more.

That was the thing about time: for an immortal like me, it meant little. Which meant I forgot about simple things like sunrises, and sunsets and what I needed to do in the darker hours.

The next morning, the ship, the tender, and all my visitors were gone.

CHAPTER TWO

BLAZE

Three full moons passed before I found another blur that crossed my horizon. This time, rather than the large ships passing along where the world curves like the faintest rainbow in a hundred shades of blue, the boat resembled a tiny grain of sand coasting along the water's surface. I watched with no small degree of envy, though it encroached faster than I expected a little white by bouncing across the waves as it carried a small team towards me.

I sat on my rock longer this time, watching them approach with the sun at my back, hopefully hiding me with its long afternoon blaze. A breeze from the sea whipped around me, and I stayed way too long until a cloud passed across the glow at my back. I slipped into the fissures beneath my feet, placing my salamander on a rock that steamed the moment he settled. Nahi looked at me inquisitively and dropped to race around my ankles excitedly.

I shook my head. "No. You're staying here. I need to go and investigate." His head tilted on an angle.

The little shit was going to follow me. I knew it, just from the way he licked the rocks and jiggled on his toes. Did all salamanders dance like that? I had no idea, seeing as I'd only met one.

That was another thing I picked up from the books. Profanity. The colorful form of language varied from age to age, but even Vikings, it appeared, cursed. It was a fun habit.

"It won't be that bad. I'll be back here before you know it, and then I'll read to you, okay?"

Nahi considered that thought, his head bouncing with his jiggles before he nodded and dashed off, a tiny fiery beacon against the island's underside.

I closed my eyes and let my body flicker into the sort of flame that flowed between the crevices, slipping beneath the surface in a mirror image too small for any human to pass through. In my other form I could only go where they did; as a flame, I was much more malleable, flickering and dancing from place to place. I drifted between broken shards of volcanic rock, twisting and turning and jittering in my own way. Just like the fire dance I performed for warriors past, letting the energy flow through my flames that swished about playfully. Like a fish I watched once in the water, still jealous that I couldn't join them and float about.

Finally, the ground opened out into a space large enough to admit my human form. I let my heat sink back from my skin to where it resided soul deep inside me. Shivers hit me in an instant. Without my magma bath or the sun's warning touch, the shadows ate at me, extinguishing my heat as I hid at the entrances to my caves just beyond the beaches. I could watch the encroaching boat here, and they couldn't see me. Which was exactly how I liked it.

Dimming my glow, I wrapped my arms around myself and chattered softly in the shade. Here, the rocks weren't warm at all, cooler than the sand in the sun. I longed to bury my feet in it, turn the tiny grains into mirror like glass with its unique twists and turns. A form of art, perhaps.

My visitors pulled their boat right up onto the beach, its bottom shallow enough to skip over the coral and coral reef that surrounded my island flourished thanks to the volcanoes, life-giving properties. That life flourished after death, the concept of something dying off in its entirety, remained forever alien to me. The cycle of the trees brewed a certain sort of mortality of its own. Growth perished on the surface, but the roots beneath survived, curling back beneath the island's cracks. Greenery shot through the blackened volcanic rock months later to cover the entire island. Prolific, and ever evolving.

Unlike me, a static flame, locked away within the confines of the sands and their imprisoning waters.

I could travel through the volcano, but I feared being stuck down there eternally beneath the surface, unable to shift my form, unable to move. Locked in a wall of rock. Fear washed over me at the thought of tight spaces with no exit and no entrance. Somewhere I would have to remain, and never find my way home.

No, the island was my home and I never wanted to leave.

Liar, liar, immortal ass on fire.

I focused on the boat, still shivering, and rubbed my body against the cave's walls, seeking heat, but there were little remnants of what I needed in cold rock. This patch of volcano stood in the shadows for too long. Frustrated, I sighed studying the bodies that jumped from the boat, pulling in the boat with the small anchor that attached itself to nothing at all. The *Mishap.*

I read the boat's name in pretty blue letters laid against the white hull. Then came their equipment, the scientists unloading all their bags and devices and cameras, all fascinated with my island, with the repercussions of the bombing that went on and on and on between the years.

Between wars.

Another thing I read about and hated. Why were people so filled with rage when a volcano or any other natural element could flatten their lives, the existence of their world, in an instant? But humanity didn't appear to think that way. As fascinated as I was with these new people and their technologies, they also terrified me. These scientists weren't like the revenant tribes with their offerings and their gifts and promises, empty as they were. The worst they could do was stab ineffectively at my flames. But these scientists… They were much more clinical, taking their samples and lining their cases with stolen pieces of my history here to study and poke and cut.

Does flame cut?

I didn't want to know the answer to that, nor did I want to find out.

Lost in my melancholy, I barely noticed the man approaching through the trees, slashing aside stunted shrubbery and scrubby bushes. My breath let out in a rush that the wind blessedly whisked away as I pressed my body to the rock, crouching down. The shadows concealed me as the stumpy, balding man stopped to undo his trousers. The stink of urine filled the air in my direction. I bent down lower, my hair, tickling my back. Dammit, I forgot to put that out. My hair had its own life and personality to match. Sweeping my hands over my head, I extinguished the last flames, cupping them in my hand. The faint smell of smoke covered urine, and I managed to breathe again.

People stink.

I breathed out as he walked away, whistling and mumbling to himself. When his footsteps faded, I shot back into the cave's welcome shadows, glancing down at myself. I'd been alone for so long, I forgot human things, like clothes. Reading wasn't the same as seeing. Sighing, I drifted in my flame form back through the rocks to my case of clothing decades old, some even centuries. Grass skirts and head-dresses that never suited *now*. I kept those simply because I could. A faded, tactile memory of tribes that no longer existed.

Moons back I managed to steal a case of the pretty semi-translucent materials that some of the female scientists wore in the water, draped around their hips, usually when they wanted to entice one of their male coworkers into their tents at night. I smiled. Some of these scientists could even rival my ancient lovers. Perhaps I could find myself the Viking warrior one day, or maybe try out one of these scientists, though their soft hands and pale faces interested me little.

I tied off this sarong around my shoulders and at me back, the material shimmering with its batik patterns, and wiggled my shoulders. Nothing untoward would fall out in the event someone saw me, though I was unused to having to cover my breasts. Or the rest of me. Most of the warriors of eons past just wanted a naked female to bed and brag about later. And in the past only grass skirts were encouraged. Maybe a few pretty leis. Now, everything was covered.

I stretched my arms in front of me, hating the way the material pinched, my armpits and loosened the ties a little, breathing out. That was better. But now I had to walk back to where I wanted to be in order to thief what I needed... craved. Hey, a girl has to have hobbies, and stealing from the scientist who came to my island was mine.

Picking up the end of the lavender and orange material, I gathered it into a knot as I started my much longer walk across the island. Human feet just didn't do it for me, I swore. By the time I made it back to the beach, the scientists had set up most of their things in neat, tidy rows. Tents in one line, tables and equipment in another. Most didn't care about their sleeping quarters, keen to get their instruments out and start measuring and poking and pruning.

I watched their activity cautiously from behind a cluster of boulders as the last left, running my hands through my hair to ensure that nothing untoward glowed. It didn't, and I edged closer. My fingers trailed the edges of waterproofed cases open on the tables. Moats were empty, their corners sharp. A quick glance around proved the camp was still deserted.

I ducked into the nearest tent, rifling quickly through one of the opened bags with its jagged odd clasps. The things I needed most–a power bank as a battery were the first things I found, along with a set of solar panels I'd seen used on a previous incursion to power things.

"Bingo."

Another good word.

Finally, *finally*, I'd be able to charge my ereader. The next bag held a better prize – an actual physical book with the same sort of cover as the ones I loved. The man had a head of hair any woman would covet, flowing over his shoulders and pecs. Ink covered tanned skin, and the woman he embraced bent backwards over his arms, swooning beautifully.

Swoon was another word I loved.

I suppose I could do the pose for a second, but my body didn't like it, and my back cracked.

Loudly.

An answering one–more like a footstep than a back–cracked outside the tent.

With my prizes clutched tightly in my arms, I crouched into the corner. There was no other sound outside as I slipped out of the tent's enclosing walls, scampering out of the camp. I rounded the safety of my boulders, and stopped.

A tall man stood in my safe zone. Not thin, exactly but not a hulk by any standards. None of the scientist's cohort were. Still, there was something about him that made me stare–and not just run for my existence.

Dressed in a white shirt, two pairs of glasses–one

on his eyes and another propped on his head over a swath of curly, dark hair. He stared at me in a mirror of my shocked expression at his appearance. Jeans hung around his legs where he stood barefoot on sand. His hand held a small device, rubbing it. But his eyes were fixed on me, dark and fathomless, like they were thirsty for something.

Me.

Clearly, too many romance novels and the occasional atlas went to my head.

His fingers worked on their own like my hair, they seemed like separate entities. One part watching, the other part always working, working, working.

A soft laugh passed his lips on a breath as I took a horrified step backward.

Away. Anywhere but here.

But still, like the tide to the shore, I was drawn back to him, step by retreated step.

One back, two forward. Reverse. The space between us shrank and widened but never closed.

Surprise lit his darkening gaze. His mouth opened, but before I could hear whatever he might say I was off, dashing through the trees and stunted shrubs, running as fast as my body carrying me. Sure, I could disappear into the cracks, sink into the island's hidden spaces, but that would mean leaving my prizes behind. What was the point of being caught if I couldn't entertain myself between visitors?

Stupid, stupid, stupid.

Running, running, running.

A small, desperate sound tore from my lips. There was no way the man would keep my existence to himself. After all, wasn't I who or what they sought, braving the waters, encroaching on my space? I dashed forward, heedless of the sticks scraping my arms, the stunted palm leaves tearing at my skin with their dry, sharp edges.

A singular thought tripped through my mind over and over.

He'll tell.

His friends will talk about what he saw.

They'll find me.

A primitive game of hide and seek with me as the prize.

No. No, no, nonononono–

What if they didn't believe him? The island was uninhabited. Everyone knew that. The world knew that. According to my atlas, my island was off limits to the people. That's why my tribes and warriors stopped coming. They even named my little rock.

Kahoolawe.

Perhaps the man's little scientist friends would think he'd had too much to drink. The liquor these pale men drank had nothing on the old tribal kava, but it still had a decent kick to it, at least for the little I managed to thief and consume, watching behind the rocks like a lizard basking in the rays of something different to its sun.

No, this man wouldn't be believed. This secret was safe between the two of us. Just us. That was all.

...*Right?*

CHAPTER THREE

SINCLAIR

I stared at the wavering tree fronds where the girl with the flames licking her hair disappeared minutes before, my mouth still hanging open. We knew the island had no inhabitants. But I also knew the legends of the Firebird. Fairytales of the older Hawaiian cultures paying homage to the volcano god who protected the villages. Even stories of human males meeting with her. Consummating their strength by taking on the passion of the girl who wore flames for clothes and could destroy civilizations in an instant.

But none of that was science, and my colleagues discarded the myths with scoffs and snobbery.

So once, might have I. I kept reading nonetheless, and on our last visit to the island, I saw something.

Sitting high at the lap of the volcano, on her highest peak. Glittering, like the sun fell to Earth. The goddess of the volcano in the flesh. Or flames. A fantastical, romantic theory that would get me laughed off the trip.

We were here to study the island and the effects of decades of bombing on the volcano's status. But that mission and my personal one no longer meshed so well. I wanted to find her. I knew she was there. I knew she was hiding.

And now, I'd seen her.

It wasn't something I could mention to my fellows, and I knew that. This part of the trip was for me alone. The government forced the need for our landing on the island, and the locals were uncomfortable already, though officials above my pay grade forced the issue and paid handsomely for our limited time ashore.

Seeing her in the flesh was literally more than I hoped. I wasn't sure if the fire girl would have a physical form other than the bright glow I noticed months before on our previous trip. And I certainly never thought I would be close enough to touch her breathing flesh...

Okay, so my research project wasn't just about the island or the legend it encompassed. She quickly became my obsession.

Strange, though, she stared at me as the object of her fear at being seen.

What's happened to you? Was I the first person to see you in...how many years, exactly?

There were no other reports of her existence for the last two hundred years or so, at least, not that I found. Perhaps she had been hiding, or sleeping. What did immortal gods do on their days off? I didn't know how long she'd been around, but I wondered if she did. The contents of her arms ran through my mind. The solar panel. The power bank.

The book.

Did gods read? The thought triggered a memory back to the last trip and our final inventory. Thanks to the military, our procedures were extra rigorous. We hadn't damaged any more equipment than usual, and there were no storms or kit washed away. The inventory had been surprisingly good. But one of the scientists admitted to losing his ereader. From the blush on his cheeks, that thing either contained some good smut, or straight out literary porn.

Now, seeing my island goddess running off with a power bank and a solar panel on an otherwise tech free chunk of volcanic rock situated in the middle of the north Pacific Ocean, I wondered at the real reasoning behind Kahoolawe's forbidden status.

Officially, the government finished bombing the island as a test site in the mid-nineties, and started clean up afterward. Nothing terribly official and the warnings to the crew on the ground–our crew–were to watch for unexploded ordnance. Perfect, as what I really wanted was to lose a limb before breakfast. The epoch was still off limits to the public, yet we were tasked with testing the stability of the land-mark and forecasting the long term effects of the military's local heyday.

Even before we left for our first run at the island–this being our second time out–the team's general consensus was that the assignment was bullshit. For a group of scientists who couldn't agree with what to make for any given meal or what cutlery to use, that was quite an achievement.

Everything about the research trip felt wrong. From the lack of equipment to the military escort in case of 'pirates', the whole thing stank of a govern-ment conspiracy, and one I wasn't familiar with.

Until I met her.

Those soft lips parted, her hair glowing around her shoulders where they curved in like she feared someone might steal her stash...but it was the eyes that lured me. Scared...lonely.

Scared of people.

Too lonely not to come near us, or just a girl and her books? Could anything be simpler?

I grinned, hustling my ass back to my work before anyone caught me gawking. Especially the military escort, though those were housed on the boat thankfully, along with all their...hardware.

A research trip that needed guns should probably be called something else.

"Sinclair. Got your kit set up?" Duncan, the lead for the trip, bustled over with his most self-important beret stuck firmly to his balding dome.

I waved my notebook at him. "Going old school for this one."

He tipped his head back in an effort to stare down his nose at me, and failed. "Shouldn't you be taking temperatures and...whatever else it is you do, Mister Kincaid?"

I blinked. The man's ability to summon pomp rivaled an arch-bishop. It was like he missed his calling.

"You want me to find a temperature gauge?"

Somewhere behind me, I swore I heard a woman laugh.

The corners of my lips curled as I fought the urge to smirk. Mostly.

"Just do your job," the rotund man all but snarled. "Three days. That's all we have. Get your readings, make your observations and we get the hell off this rock."

I frowned. "I thought this was a three week trip."

"Three. Days."

My head wasn't the only one that jerked. Across the beach, Jordie and Sam, our resident British paleontologist and his same-science husband, both paused with their hands stuck in the dirt.

Getting acquainted.

We were promised more time on the island.

What the fuck changed?

And why did we have a mountain of food in the small boat that barely contained us all? I muttered to myself, pushing my boots into the sand that fast turned to extrusive igneous rock, making up most of the island's outer structure. Around us, divots in the surface exhibited the island's volatile history, a heady mix of human violence warring against the best and worst mother nature offered.

Or maybe a fire girl as bright as the sun.

I followed the path she set unconsciously, or maybe with her in mind as I traipsed into the island's interior, keeping my feet careful. Our drone flight from a prior trip showed a large crater filled with water like a lagoon at one end, but I headed deeper, toward the peak. I wouldn't make it all the way today, if I ever got there at all, should Duncan's timeline be believed.

"So much fucking wrong with this trip. This place..." I muttered, my thoughts fragmenting as I noted the heat exchange between air and ground temperature under foot, watching for the unexploded bombs.

We were given a strict set of paths to tread on an unspecified mud map, but that wouldn't save my life if I didn't keep an eye out or something buried beneath the surface chose that moment to give me a chance to see if I was wrong about my theories on god.

For the moment I'd say I was squarely in the negative, all because of a girl who shouldn't exist where she did.

Or look the way she does.

I was so keen to get away from Duncan's creepy as fuck stare, and the guns at my back all the while praying I didn't have a dot lasered through my shirt, and only a little obsessed about the island goddess that I didn't see the geyser between the rock fissures

I jumped over, hidden between the swirls and crevices.

Only the flicker of flame where it shouldn't be, lurching upward from the volcanic surface toward me.

Flame that transformed into those panicked, pretty as fuck pink eyes I recognized at once.

Stopping and staring saved my life and sealed my fate.

My impossible vision was followed by a hiss and an eruption that, had I been two steps forward, would have flung my body forty feet straight up–and straight back down onto the blackened stone and its sparse overgrowth.

All that happened to me was I was knocked backwards by the deluge of surprisingly cold water. I registered that, and the warm hand that gripped mine, rising impossibly through the crevices where no human should be.

Right before the back of my head contacted the igneous rock, and my world turned as black as the stone beneath me.

CHAPTER FOUR

BLAZE

The scientist I pulled off Kahoolawe's most random geyser stirred at my feet. I swore the spirit that inhabited its pipes had a one thousand year PMS cycle, but the damn creature refused to talk to me no matter how often I bugged it. Not that the revelation was surprising.

Erupting right when I found a prime specimen to play with was beyond annoying.

My flaming hair scared most of the not-locals away in the years gone by, and as my island claimed a 'forbidden' status for the past near two hundred years of war, experiments and barrenness, my social starvation reached an epic high.

In the past, I was wooed by island and Hawaiian

warriors who risked the wrath of my shores in search of the fire goddess who inhabited the rock I sat upon, sacrificing themselves for a chance to stoke my...um...fires.

Not really. I mean, they went home a little dazed, but fully intact. Kind of. I'd never been *that* kind of monster. Which was how I ended up seeing out my own mini-sacrifice after what felt like an eon of abstinence while my flame burned on alone.

Flying solo wasn't anything like what it was cracked up to be.

I stroked my fire salamander's back, sinking into myself as the heat from his flames emanated into my fingers and along my arm. "Sinny-Sinclair," I cooed, poking the nerdy, goofy and oh-so-freaking cute scientist in his dark denim and black t-shirt with my toe. "It's time to wake *upppp*."

Dark framed eyes popped open, displaying a dazed kind of intelligence that quickly rose to the challenge I set with my foot on his chest, perched on my hot rock above him. Sinclair Kincaid's mouth fell open as he stared up at me, tracing his gaze from my toes resting on his chest, sliding along my legs and higher, his shock morphing into hunger in an instant.

"Sin-clairrrr," I sang again, and he winced.

Okay, so my singing voice could use some work. It's not like I had an audience to tell me I was too pitchy.

Sinclair tried to push himself up, but I kept my toes right where they were–in the center of his chest–and pushed him back. He reclined on his elbows, studying the exposed skin of my body, seeking the shadows where my flaming, strawberry blond hair curled around my thighs, concealing the rest of me from his sight.

No clothes this time. I was sick of the damn things. Which left just enough skin on display to tease, but not touch. For right now, that put us at a little impasse I wanted him to break straight through. If he had the courage.

In the past the only champions to land on my shores were the hulking, man cave sort–literally, for that era of humanity. Pushed into their position by their girth or the village's need for a blessing. But times changed, and perhaps I could, too. Besides, I had slightly ulterior motives, but my tame sexy nerd-boy didn't need to know that just yet.

"I saw you," he blurted as his gaze licked over my face like the first hopeful flicker from a simmering ember, "Outside the cave, where I was working. I saw you. You were…"

"Soooo sizzling hot." I fanned myself.

My salamander went out.

Oops.

I tapped Nahi's back, and the little fire lizard combusted in a glowy blue ball of insane heat that soaked deep to my ravenous core that was always hungry for warmth. He turned in circles on my knee, nested in my hair that hung past my ass, and fell asleep. His glow subsided to a flurry of pretty orange flames I waved my fingers through.

"I– I don't have a gift for you." He searched his pockets and came up with a tattered tissue and a stretchy black little ring.

I smiled, not answering, glad he clicked on to the program about islands and goddesses and the proper way to worship.

"That doesn't hurt you, does it?" Sinclair's gaze sharpened, lighting just over Nahi's head.

"No…" I glanced down. My breasts were exposed by the lizard's nesting habits.

Biting my lips, I unwound the little lizard carefully, settling him on the steamy rock at my back and tossed my hair over my shoulder. "Is that view better?"

My pet scientist licked his lips. "What's your name?"

I laughed at him. "You have a naked fire goddess playing footsies with you, and you want to know my *name*?"

He shrugged, dragging his gaze to my face with effort. "Names are important. You seem to know mine, and it definitely holds power over me. Isn't that how these sorts of stories go?" He gestured around his waist where an impressive tent bulged out from his jeans.

"That looks painful," I murmured, looking down at him through my lashes.

I stroked my toes across his chest. The soft cotton of his tee pulled tight over planes of hidden muscle. My grin turned wicked. Perhaps my geek had more than just one secret.

"Almost." He closed his eyes as I edged my toes lower. "If I touch you, will I burn?"

"Was that meant to be a cliché?" I raised both eyebrows, letting my flame go out.

Darkness fell over us, the volcanic glass cave illuminated only by Nahi's soft glow.

"No. I've never met a goddess before."

Sinclair didn't move, but now we were clothed in darkness and shadows, he took the time to rake his gaze over me. His eyes hooded and he let out a long, controlled breath.

"How do you know I'm a goddess?" I wasn't, but what other term was humanity to use around creatures they couldn't explain who lived long beyond their brief mortal splash in the pool of eternal existence?

"Because I want to fall on my knees and worship you," Sin whispered.

I sighed softly. *He is the perfect choice.* "You will make a beautiful sacrifice," I informed him.

His lips curled up. "I can't think of a better way to die."

"You're supposed to be shocked."

He considered me, and raised one hand slowly, hovering his fingers over my foot. Just as slowly, watching me every second for my reaction, he glided his fingertips over my toes, stroking along to my ankle and back again.

Just once. Not an inch more.

Then his hand dropped.

"How long has it been since you had contact with another...being?" He swallowed as I dug my toes into his stomach.

Nice amount of muscle there, too.

The lean sort, not the bulging, showy type.

"Too long," I murmured. "Why aren't you running and screaming, little scientist? I don't fit into your tightly categorized world. Imprisoned. Poked. Barbarized." I met his sort over the centuries, those who wanted to draw and dissect and label and name everything they touched. Including me.

Not all of them left my island.

Which was why I was so resistant in giving him mine.

I didn't want to become another static bug encased in a glass prison, pinned and spread out for study, to burn on demand.

I wanted someone to burn for me, at my call.

Someone I wanted to burn for.

"Is that a word?" He considered me through narrowed eyes. "Why would someone hide or take you? You're a person."

"And if I wasn't? If my form wasn't pleasing, if I wasn't female and brought mortal men to their knees. What then, scientist? Would you put me in a case and display me at your mausoleums?" I frowned.

"Museums." Sinclair Kincaid laughed. "You have a fascinating knowledge of a world when I think you were born long ago. Am I wrong?"

"No," I said idly, stroking Nahl's flames. "I have seen humanity change and yet not over too many eons to count. I won't hurt you if you're nice to me, you know."

"How many have hurt you?" He frowned, his face darkening. "You exist. You have a right to be free."

"So many you've never heard about." Or maybe he had. The humans had a way of transporting information from one person to the next. "They used to bomb my shores. Practice, they called it. Blowing holes in my home. An effort to keep me contained. And then...nothing. They closed me off from the rest of the world. Once, twice a year maybe, I see your type. But I've never spoken to a scientist before."

None let me, before they used their nets and harpoons and guns to pin me down.

That situation turned out poorly for all involved.

"I'll try to uphold my breed before you turn my bones to ash," he said dryly.

I laughed. "You are too cute, Sinny-Sinclair. Tell me, would you go willingly to your death to touch me again?" I flickered flame from my fingers, letting their sweet caress lick at my skin.

His eyes followed the flame's intimate flickers with a ravenous hunger that left me hotter than any fire could burn.

"Yes," he whispered.

"Then touch me, human man. If you dare." I

trailed my toes over his belt, tracing the thin strap of leather there.

"Tell me your name," he insisted, his voice straining as I caressed his bulge with the arch of my foot. A groan left his lips, and he pushed his hips up into my touch.

"Hunaahi is what they used to call me. But in your language, I think my name is...Blaze."

"Blaze. It fits. A little cliché, perhaps..." He gasped as I steamed his jeans just enough for my heat to warm him, no more.

"Is it wise to snark at the foot that burns, little scientist?"

"But if you burn me away, you'll be left alone. I know you don't want that." He panted a little, then his hand came down on my ankle, squeezing tight for a second before he released me. Breath hissed between clenched teeth.

I yanked my foot away, curling both legs beneath myself as I peered down at him. "Why did you do that? Crazy boy," I tsked from my perch.

He knelt before me. "You asked if I would burn to touch you, be your sacrifice. I told you the truth."

My breath came fast as he held out his hand etched with the pattern of my flames. Whorls and eddies that obliterated the natural markings of his palm gave him pain, and yet he endured it.

For me.

I placed my own hand over his, taking the heat back into me. His body would remember the sensation, but it wouldn't sting any more, the way I learned humans did at my touch.

"You're nothing like what I expected." Leaning forward, I dipped my head until our breaths mingled.

His sweet, like a mixture of fruits. Mine clean and hot.

"You are exactly how I expected you to be," he whispered back. Without raising a hand, he pushed up on his knees and pressed his mouth to mine, risking my wrath and his entire existence for a kiss.

My heart seared in my chest at his touch, but I didn't fight him. Sinclair offered soft kisses, firm but not demanding. He explored me with lips and tongue, tasting and dancing while my inner flame grew molten. His tongue swept into my mouth, discovering everything I held back until I was heady with a lack of air, and tumbled forward off my rock.

Gravity encompassed me as I fell, and I remembered to draw my flame in at the last moment before he caught me.

Strong arms wound around my body. Sinclair Kincaid was not the weedy little man I thought when I first caught him studying samples with his tiny machines on my shores, and later walking where he shouldn't be. When I first heard his name.

No, this man, this human was the ultimate surprise. He held me tight, his body folding around mine like a sling to prevent me from hitting the hard obsidian glass floor of my cave.

"I could have killed you," I gasped, turning in his arms.

Had I not withdrawn my heat, I would be a dragon in a fairytale, with a knight's ash beneath me. It was amazing the stories I collected, both spoken and written over the years.

All of them told the same: an immortal and a human never worked out.

Any of my past lovers would have been over me in an instant, taking what they could before my flame reignited to end their short lives. Or they left me with their empty promises, and I was alone, again.

"But you didn't. And it would have been my fault you hurt." He stroked my hair back from my face, his eyes fixed on mine. Greens and browns shot through each other there, a maelstrom of forest and earth, grounding me.

I curled in his arms, shivering. "I'm not used to this."

"Touch? A connection? You must have been so lonely, Blaze." His use of my name sent a shot of aching need through my glass heart, melting and reforming it in a moment.

"Am I just another fascination for you?"

Sinclair stared down at me. "No, fire girl. You're so much more than that for me. I begged to worship you, revere you, and I'll keep asking." His mouth found mine in a slow, long kiss that left me burning from the inside out.

What else could a goddess ask?

"Fine, you can stay," I murmured.

Until I need to leave. Then you'll take me with you.

However long he needed to come to that conclusion, I'd keep him.

But when I slid my hands under his shirt, Sin caught my wrists, tugging them free from his skin.

"Don't you want..?" I frowned at the conundrum he presented. "Everyone else did."

"I am not everyone else," he said firmly, finding his jacket and sliding it over my shoulders.

The scent of him encompassed me, the material

hanging to my knees. "No one has ever dressed me before." I frowned. "This form has always been pleasing."

"Oh, you're plenty pleasing." His fingers lingered at my waist, frustratingly refusing to edge either higher or lower while I thrummed from within. "But right now I need to think."

I leaned into his space and bopped my nose on his. "You don't use your brain for this one, little scientist."

His gaze latched onto mine and I saw what he denied himself in those green flickering depths. "That's what I'm worried about. I want to earn your love, your respect, goddess. How else does a mortal commit to an everlasting heart, and not be tossed aside like your past lovers?"

"Who said I tossed them aside?" I pulled back from his chest, but his arms wound around me, tangling me in cloth and scents and him. "They sailed from my shores, not the other way around."

And not one of them took me with them.

But I didn't say that, because with Sin, I didn't need to. For the first time in a dozen millennia, someone listened. A favor I found all too easy to return. A trust given. Risked.

"I won't leave you."

"You can't promise me that." I frowned, not liking the conversation's twists and turns.

I wanted off my island. He was my ticket. I'd be everything he desired. What more did either of us need than that?

At some point he would run. But like the princess in the fairytale, I'd chase. Or maybe that was the dragon's part. I only read that once, and wasn't sure I liked the ending.

"I gave you my word, Blaze." His hands tightened on my lower back, jerking me into him until my body molded to his.

I scraped my hands over his tee. "Clothes are not my favorite thing." Tilting my head back, I grazed my mouth along his chin, delighting in the rough stubble there. "Tell me what you want, Sin."

His groan sated my need, knowing I could bring him pleasure.

And I had plenty to give.

CHAPTER FIVE

SINCLAIR

"I want..." I trailed off, lost in those glowing magenta eyes that matched her flaming hair as it rose around her in a halo, a sign of her intent, or passion? I didn't know but by every rule of this earth I knew to be true and all the ones that disintegrated just from being near her, I wasn't sure what I wanted, other than to be with her. "I want to know what you want, Blaze."

She watched me through her lashes for a long breath as her body heated in my arms. Sweat beaded my torso, drenched my jeans, but I didn't care.

I lied. I knew exactly what I wanted. To kiss her until the sun rose and then kiss her some more. To take her off this rock, swim with her in the cool waters surrounding it, and take her home. To my home. But my small apartment wasn't designed to fit an immortal fire goddess. Nor was my life. Besides, what did I have to offer her that she couldn't take for herself?

She's lonely.

"What I want?" she asked slowly, as though testing the words out for the first time. "Why would you need to know that?"

I frowned. "The others really left you, didn't they?" I tipped her chin up when she hid from me, her hair forming a wave of curls and flames between us. "Let me see you," I whispered.

"So you can put me in a bottle and take me home?"

Home. That's exactly where I wanted to take her. The truth of her accusation struck me square in the chest, and that instant broke something in her. Her eyes searched mine, and she shoved at my chest, freeing herself.

"No, not like that!" I choked, lunging for her and catching only scraps of flame tips that seared my fingers. "I do want to take you home but, Blaze–"

"No *buts*!" she cried, whirling around in a maelstrom of fire and light. "I knew you'd just want to test me and poke me and prod me and- and- cut me into tiny pieces and-"

"Stew you?" I asked wryly, sitting back on my haunches.

"Well... I can't cook." She shrugged like it was nothing, like her crisis hadn't burst out of her.

"You're a lonely immortal and are unsure of your place in a new world," I murmured, knowing instinctively I was right.

She squinted at me. "Aren't you supposed to be all numbers and analytics?"

"How do you know so much about the world?" I tipped my head to one side when she flung a tablet at me that revealed several reading apps filled with bodice rippers. "Ahh. This is your take on our world? All fiery passions that suit you, and unrequited love?"

She sniffed. "I don't think there's anything quiet about those women or their men."

A laugh bubbled up from me. "No, there probably isn't." I held out a hand. "Will you come sit with me and talk again? I liked having you close." My cheeks burned in a way that had nothing to do with her heat and everything to do with mine. "We were talking about what you wanted."

She crawled hesitantly across to me, and I lifted

her onto my lap without thinking, like it was the most natural place for her to be. Blaze swung her legs over my hips, squeezing my thighs with the insides of hers.

"You are different," she acknowledged softly, tracing heated paths along my chest.

"Says the fire girl straddling my lap naked," I muttered.

"Does that make you uncomfortable?" Her head tilted to one side as she assessed me.

"Not unless you mean in the way that makes me want to pin you to the floor and ravish you," I admitted freely. "Only, I'm not likely to be doing much ravishing."

"Why not?" Her brow crinkled like I just delivered the worst insult in the world.

I smiled gently. "I'm a virgin, Blaze. A harmless sort of side effect of being a workaholic whose idea of a date is studying thermodynamics of an island no one's supposed to be on."

"You studied my island?" Her mouth popped into a small 'o'. "That's...sweet. I've never had someone study my home before."

"It's an interesting place." I curbed the desire to deluge her with the readings of this place that seemed so unusual–and now I knew why. "I think you missed my point, Sun Star."

"Sun Star?" She nibbled her lip, staring down at me while her hair rose on its own around her shoulders, the ends glowing and alight, fluttering around her shoulders.

I frowned. "Hasn't anyone given you a nickname before?"

"No, Sinny-Sinclair, no one has named me before," she snapped, her eyes blazing as she stared down at me. Her hips undulated in a rhythm that left me breathless. "And I've never had a problem with a lover before. I'm sure I've got enough experience in fucking for the both of us."

I grinned, winding my fingers through her hair, enjoying the light pain on the backs of my knuckle where her flaming hair nipped at me. "Those romance books have done a number on you haven't they? What else is on this list of expectations that I can't stand up to?"

She laughed softly, lowering her mouth to mine as I massaged her nape. "Let's find out together."

Her mouth was soft and warm as she kissed me lightly, then more firmly. Insistent.

"Whoa." I pressed my hands to her shoulders

and pulled her back a little. "I promised you we wouldn't go too fast.'

She huffed at me. "You asked me what I want, and *this* is what I want, Sinclair. Right now." She tipped her head to one side. "And maybe to leave my island. But not be banished from it."

"I can understand that and I'm not sure I can promise you anything," I said softly, seeking the disappointment sure to rise in her face. "I can try to get you off the island, but I'm on a boat full of military men with no women and that's going to be a tough mission. Unless you can shrink into a box or something," I murmured, watching her. "That was you in those crevices, wasn't it? Before the geyser."

She nodded slowly. "Yes, and I can, but enclosed spaces make me..." She shuddered, a full body effort that displayed her all too real fear of the process.

"Maybe just for a short time. A few days?" I caught her chin and pulled her mouth back to mine. "Maybe I can rethink the promise of no sex."

"Good."

Her hair flung back in a pink tinged halo that lit her entire being, her arms curling around my neck. "Show me how these pants work, Sinny-Sinclair."

"Jeans."

"Jeans." She rolled the word around her mouth as though tasking it for the first time.

I swallowed hard as her hips moved with her. "Christ, Blaze. That's–" Air trapped in my lungs and refused to budge. "I think I need to start with exploring you or this won't last long at all."

Her smile turned wicked. "You liked how I felt before..." She wiggled on my lap.

I bit back a groan. "Does my little Sun Star have a foot fetish?"

"Maybe?" She looked disconcerted at the term and shrugged. "Let's find out."

Before I could get a hand to my zip, she swung around on my lap, pushing me back to the ground a bit awkwardly and placed her feet–and her pretty pink and glistening pussy–right in my face.

"Blaze–"

"Use that mouth of yours, Sinclair," she instructed, working on my belt with nimble fingers then playing with my zip, working it up and down. "Oh, this is fun."

"Never seen jeans or a zip before?" I tried to ignore the pussy in my face and caught her foot in my palm, running my tongue over her arch.

I nearly blew in my pants before she exposed my cock to the air that seemed heavier than before at the moan that elicited from her lips when I played with her feet. Those warm, soft lips that grazed over my cock through my tighty whities.

Her toes curled with each flick of my tongue as I worked my way across the side of her foot, discovering which areas made her sigh, and which made her moan, creating a Blaze shaped catalogue in my mind with all her favorite things listed, and a pair of glowing eyes just like hers.

She lowered her mouth my cock. Let out a groan, I bit down lightly on her toe and lost myself in her kisses.

"Hasn't anyone given you pleasure before Sinny Sinclair?" she asked.

"I've done everything but actually have sex." I managed, sucking on the tips of her toes. *Perfect.* She ground down against me as I worked my way around her ankles, along those calves to her thighs. Her breath came faster, and she growled over her shoulder at me. "What's her name, and who do I have to kill?"

"You're the only one that asked me that."

One glimpse of her, and I was smitten. Weren't mortals supposed to fear deities? If you believed in such legends and suddenly, I found myself on the other side of the fence as a true believer.

She huffed cutely, blowing her hair over her shoulder, and baring her back to me. Looking forward, I slid my tongue across her pussy, tasting her properly for the first time. I gripped the perfectly round globe of her ass, my other sliding along her back to push her down onto me. The noises that came from her did me in. I ate her like she wanted – ravished, worshiped, even loved. Was love possible with the goddess? It wasn't like anyone else would come close after her.

Panting. She pushed my pants down, sliding her mouth around the head of my cock and didn't stop until her nose pressed against my balls.

I choked on sweet pussy, and decided it was the perfect way to die.

Legs wrapped around the sides of my head, and she rode me gently, rocking her mouth over me with the same unfaltering rhythm she had when she sat on my lap, rubbing herself against my cock. Was there anything more arousing in the world than having a naked girl on my lap, and while I was close to fully closed, letting me touch her and tasting her? My cock in her mouth pressed to the back of her throat. I molded my mouth to her pussy, swirling my tongue around her gorgeous flesh, soothing and teasing and licking and loving. I found her clit and sucked gently.

It didn't take long before we were both on edge. I gripped her ass with both hands, pulling her tight against my mouth, but she shook against me, wiggling fast.

I released her. "Did I hurt you? Do you want more of something?"

"No. I want to come with you inside me," she whispered breathlessly.

"Granted." With a surge of energy I didn't understand I slid my hand along her spine, sitting up suddenly and kissing the back of her neck. I rolled us both until I arched over her, kicking my pants free. I grabbed my t-shirt and ripped it over my head. "I might not be the sort of golden glowing warrior that –"

Her eyes glowed as her palms skated down my chest over the ink wrapped around my ribs, stating the first law of thermodynamics, that energy couldn't be created, nor destroyed, but only change form written there in curlicue.

"Shush, Sinclair. You're perfect."

I braced my hands either side of her head, dipping my mouth to kiss her, letting her taste herself on my tongue.

Her moan was softer, this time, her breath shorter as I nudged her thighs, parted her entrance.

"Do I need to pray to you, worship, or beg?" I stared at her seriously. If my first time was going to be with a goddess, then I wanted to get it right. That was what I wanted. For her.

Like I said, belief systems effectively shifted.

Shook her head, her lips parting. No. Now."

The word slipped past me. She reached behind me, grabbed my ass, and pulled me closer. Her knees bent, and her heels pressed where her hands vacated, urging me forward.

No longer letting fear guide me, I surged forward. The warmth of her enveloped me, taking me to a place deep inside her.

Her body arch to accommodate me, her pussy fluttering prettily against my cock.

"Oh, my–" Her eyelashes fluttered, a sigh leaving her lips as her body softened, wrapping firmly around me. "Deeper.."

"Anything you want, Sun Star."

I thrust fully into her, flexing my hips as our bodies melded together. Her heat increased but I kept going, worshiping her with the heat of the volcano around us. Or maybe that was just her. But she never lost control, she never burned or seared me. Her body tightened almost painfully as she came and screamed.

The sound ricocheted off the glassed walls in fractured cries. I slammed my hips into her, flesh slapping flash, and came hard. Sweat poured off me like I ran a marathon, but her body welcomed my weight in her soft curves. I rested my head against her shoulder, breathing in her sweat, flicking my tongue out to lick the droplets from the slender column of her neck.

And when she wrapped her arms around my neck, squeezing firmly, our breaths merging in the sort of kiss that lasted both of too brief a time and an eternity at once, I knew my Sun Star was the only woman for me.

I drew back, breaking the kiss, needing fresh air before I passed out on her. Sweet words teetered on my lips, but none of them fell out, thankfully, as they probably would've been corny as fuck.

But she solved that problem for me, tipping her head back to staring into my eyes. Slow, satisfied, the smile curved her lips, and her body undulated around me. Her lashes lowered and she begged on a purr.

"Do that to me again, Sinclair."

I strode back to the campsite, scribbling notes that meant nothing frantically on my pad as evidence I knew I'd need for when Duncan literally sprang out in of me from beneath a waist height shrub.

"Jesus. Do you do that to all the guys?" I diverted my eyes in case he was doing up his jeans, but Duncan seemed to be literally waiting behind a bush for me to walk past.

"Where have you been, Mister Kincaid?" he asked with narrow eyes, his greedy, bulging eyes zeroing in on my notebook. "Show me."

"No. They're observations and my personal shorthand that won't make any sense." I pocketed my pen and my pad, brushing my hand across the front of my jeans in case it was my fly that was done.

"And what...observations did you make?" Duncan folded his arms, resting them across his chest.

"That it's quiet here. Hot." I willed myself to keep my sarcasm to myself and walk around him, determined to reclaim the perfectly ruined fantasy of Blaze wrapped around me.

"*It's quiet?*" He mocked me. Silence fell between us before Duncan ruined my virtual orgasm a second time. "Well. Did you see anything unexpected?"

"Iguanas." *A motherfucking glowing one.*

Duncan snickered at my pre-prepared line. I didn't.

I had an idea that my absence would be noted, and someone would interrogate me. I needed those answers prepped and ready. I just didn't expect it to be the self-indulgent research lead who checked me out.

"Glad you found the wildlife distracting. Keep an eye out for something that might...compromise the trip. The safety of the crew."

Pretty words, and reasonable from anyone else. But Duncan never cared a whit about whether there were tripping hazards or other minor inconveniences, as long as he got the job done. Or rather, that we did, and he got the accolades.

"Noted." I was pretty sure the military presence would be the ones taking up the hard line on crew *safety.* I pivoted to face him, forcing a smile. "What did you find?"

Duncan kept walking, making his way through the scrub that was almost as tall as him. The beach opened out in front of us. "Oh, I saw some things. "

My heart was in my throat as I followed him.

"That's nice." I said, nonchalantly. In my head I kept a running tally of the books I needed to download onto a new device for Blaze. "What spectacle made your day?" If I kept this up any longer, I'd choke on my own lies.

My gaze drifted to the cracks in the island's rock stratum searching for her tell-tale colors. I knew she was nearby, hiding, despite my begging her to stay back in the caves. My stomach flopped uneasily in my belly. The island might be forbidden. She might even be the reason for it, and if Duncan got his hands on her... A tiny glass jar and an unbreakable lid would be the least of her worries. I had to find a way to get safety off the island.

The mental image of her in my bed at home stole my breath for a full minute and I missed Duncan's next ramble.

"...unusual. Like something fell from it, all full of smoke. Pressurized."

I stubbed my boot in the sandy beach where it transformed from hard rock so hard I could've taken the skin off to the bone. "Yeah?" I tried to sound interested but at this point I didn't have the conversational skills of Blaze's little gecko. Hell, I even heard her sassing me in my thoughts in her voice.

"Do we have to worry about dragons?" I attempted a joke that fell worse than flat.

"If only it were that simple." Duncan left me with an enigmatic smile, but not before giving me a hard side eye that left me worried about what he saw, and how fucked we were.

I had to find a way to get off the island without getting either of us shot.

Fuck, fuck, fuckity fuck.

CHAPTER SIX

CHAPTER FIVE

BLAZE

I watched Sinclair talk with his friend – or maybe they weren't friends from the way they snapped at each other like so many seagulls fighting over another bird.

Or perhaps I was the one they were fighting over. Either way, his friend gave me the creeps. Nahi sneaked up onto my shoulder, caressing my cheek with tiny feet and blue flames. I cupped my hands around him as he started to glow. Playing peekaboo with these men wasn't on my to-do list. That was another term I learned from one of my stolen books.

Sinclair promised to come back tomorrow for a

sunrise breakfast if he could get away. We both knew he had limited time left on the island, do whatever job he was supposed to do. His work wouldn't allow him to be alone forever. But he might spare a few hours, and I had to come up with a plan of how to leave this place.

My collection of trinkets called to me as I scooped Nahi off my shoulder and let him run around the top of the case, running my fingers over an ornate headdress, its palm fronds drooping sadly. "Will you be able to come with me? I think maybe we will set his house alight."

Part of me desperately wanted to see Sinclair's home.

Part of me was terrified of being chopped into pieces.

Such a pleasant thought.

His voice tripped through my head. "And stewed?" I loved his twisted sense of humor that matched so closely to mine. He wasn't scared of me. He hadn't run. And...he was at least as brave as the last warriors who breached my shores.

My solar panel has been charging all day. I managed to push it through a crack above the cave while Sinclair steadied it from the outside. It might glint at surface level, but no more than any other metal left on the destroyed surface of my island. Eventually, I would have to clean and wash it. But it powered up nicely to charge my ereader and that was what I wanted most right now. It was. Definitely.

I'd found the case after a ship wrecked on my small reef a small eon ago, waiting until the tide was low enough for me to touch the soggy leather without turning blue. Nothing of its contents survived bar a piece of paper with two people's blurred faces and tatty, matted lump that might have been considered clothes once. But once I dried the case out, I stowed my headpieces and medallions and my grass skirts in it. Protected a little from the heat and in the coolest section of my cave, the case preserved my treasures.

My only worry would be if the volcano erupted, but I didn't think that would happen for a long time, if ever. For this one to spew its contents on the world the ground would have to shift and move significantly. My feet spoke of its sleep, and my island would remain for now.

But not forever.

No. The idea of escaping the island with Sinclair Kincaid drew me back to the case. I closed its lid reverently, the lingering memories obliterated by the newcomer to my life who kissed so sweetly, and played with me like he had the experience of a hundred women.

And, of course, that delicious cock of his.

Sinclair was a virgin. Maybe I was desperate. Maybe I was lonely, but he was very teachable. And he worshiped me like it was an erotic game we played, one he needed to win.

The blessing of power gave me my books back, but my ereader wasn't full of just historical women and their wild men. Sometimes the books were set in the *now* world, with its new language and people from everywhere living in huge villages, always so busy, busy, busy. Men, it seemed, still ruled this generation with their hard bodies and minds. I thought that should be the other way around, but the world is strange and matriarchal and opposing patriarchal societies merged over the eons until I was born with the seemingly necessary push and pull. One always gave way to the other eventually, and then people's values would flip with the new trend that never lasted.

Sinclair...didn't seem the same.

You're desperate.

Okay, so I'd known him for all of a day but when one date was your normal benchmark you learned to understand people's intentions in a brief, albeit powerful period.

So I'm lonely. Check.

My flame subdued as I settled back into the corner of my cave, running my fingers over the newest trophy addition to my collection. Sinclair's jacket. I traced the leather with trembling hands, the garment's scent eliciting reminders of his brand of love. And it had a zip, which he showed me how to use. That was fun too, for a brief period.

My hand fell to my side, bumping an old, irregular shaped and hand crafted slab jar. A crack traced down one side. Nothing remained in it. The perfumes and oils it once held were long used up. But the container itself could be useful.

I gripped one side, studying its almost perfect looking surface. *That won't do.* If Sinclair or his friends were to believe it was a relic to take off my island, it couldn't look like it was created yesterday. I pressed it to the hard, blackened glass and scraped it down the surface, damaging both. One side, then the other, until finally a few chips fell off. The jar looked worn and used, not like the day was gifted to me four hundred years ago. Time, like people, changed and the way the villages kept count of the seasons varied. I was still learning this new world of Sinclair's. It both terrified and fascinated me.

Satisfied with my work, I placed the jar near the entrance tunnel, picked up my fully charged ereader. There were hours to go before I could see Sinclair again, but he wanted me not to visit him in the camp at night, though I begged him for the privilege.

That was a turnabout in itself. Me, begging. Me, desperate. Maybe that last one wasn't quite so unusual after all. Making a nest in Sinclair's jacket, I clicked through the books available on ereader my until I found my favorite Viking, and immersed myself in the world where enemies lost their heads or their hearts, conflicts and minor battles were fought over land and love and lives.

That time seemed so much simpler than today. If only Sinclair could be a Viking and I his fire girl...

"So this is your quiet place."

I tugged my eyes open, the cave dimly illuminated by my muted glow. "Sinclair," I whispered, reaching for him.

"You purr as you wake up."

My eyes opened enough to drink him in where

he crouched in front of me, his arms resting on the volcanic glass shelf where I laid on my side. His jacket spread out beneath me, my ereader was tucked to my chest. I apparently cuddled it through the night after falling asleep, though my dreams weren't of a buff Viking with blonde hair and broad shoulders, but of the lanky scientist, with his dark head, who worshiped me with his mouth.

I could have his heart.

I thought we might get there, maybe, one day? He was the only one who came back, after all.

He came back.

A broad smile spread over my face, and I launched at him, pulling my flames back just in time to avoid incinerating the poor boy.

Sinclair ducked, my not in time to avoid my body clashing into his. Our temples bumped.

"Owwww." We both rubbed our foreheads.

"I brought you food. I... wasn't sure what you liked. It's pretty poor fare."

I studied the collection of treats he brought with him. "It looks wonderful." My stupid smile just wouldn't quit. "I have a solution to our problem. "

I traded a piece of dried fruit for my damaged jar.

Sinclair studied the item, tracing over the old

crack and the new marks. "Do you want me to present this to the archaeological team?" he asked, raising both eyebrows.

"To your team? I shook my head. "No. This is what you take off the island in. My...transportation."

Sinclair jerked a little as he continued to study the jar in my hands without touching it more than necessary. "Good work. What else have you got lying around?"

My eyes narrowed. "You're going to take my things, aren't you?"

Sinclair shook his head, laughing. "Nothing so devious. I need to have a reason to be here, catalogue a few things so I can keep wandering about the island." Something rang not quite truthful behind his eyes, but the happiness in his face did.

I could detect a lie without my salamander's approval and right now he glowed a fiery crimson warning.

"What's happened?" I demanded, my voice sharp in the cave's confines.

He shook his head, his eyes lighting up again. "Nothing. I brought you a gift."

Not my Sinclair. Don't lie to me. Pretty please, Sinny Sinclair.

I would still use him as my passage off the island.

But after that... my heart wanted to shatter into a million pieces. I smiled back, my eyes mistrustful. "Like what?"

Sinclair knelt at my feet trailing soft kisses along my ankles. "This." He passed me a second device that looked similar to my first. "Four hundred and eighty books." He shrugged. "It's all I had time to download with our shitty reception before the sun rose again."

I didn't flick the ereader on or brighten its screen to see what he downloaded. Instead I studied him carefully, taking notes of the deep shadows beneath his eyes, the red veins spread through his eyes. "You stayed up all night, putting books on this for me to read?"

I curved my body to be closer to his. After all the trinkets I was presented with, I'd never been gifted books before, the one thing I wanted almost as much as to get off the island. This, this right here was my new favorite thing in the world.

"Yeah," Sinclair mumbled tiredly, rubbing the back of his neck.

His cheeks stained a cute shade that matched Nahi's glow that muted as I reached out to trace my fingers along Sinclair's cheek.

I put the ereader down carefully and tucked it

into his jacket. Then I launched myself back at his face and peppered his mouth with kisses as he laughed and wound his arms around me.

"Thank you, thank you, thank you."

"Glad you like it." He kissed me back sweetly.

"You're cute." I kissed his mouth in a frenzy that grew heated fast, and not by my flames.

His hands wound through my hair, squeezing, tugging, my flames nipping at his wrists until he ground his body against mine in a dance I understood perfectly.

"You horny little thing," he muttered against my mouth on a soft groan as I rubbed my body against his.

I tucked that new term away for later, too.

"Is that bad?" I peered up through my lashes playfully.

We both knew he'd be the one on his back shortly.

"You know I like it," he said roughly.

His kiss deepened, his tongue slicing into my mouth as I pushed him down onto his back and straddled his hips with no complaint, pushing his jeans aside until I encountered bare skin. He risked my hair's wrath, fisting the strands in his hand as we rolled and rocked together until pleasure ran through our veins.

Afterwards, I didn't move, still breathless and savoring the simple need to be close to another source of warmth, our hearts beating together. Then, when he recovered enough to addict me to the feel of his hard length inside me, he had me again. We talked like animals in the heart of the island a second time.

Then again.

CHAPTER SEVEN

SINCLAIR

Day three on the island, our final day on our truncated research trip, was officially the worst fucking day of my week.

Because it wasn't Duncan who got me out of bed to get moving. It was the fucking military.

I didn't see Blaze, or manage to have any contact with her, and at the rate the military was packing us up and moving us along, there was no chance I'd get to go back to her cave.

Nor, with the largest ship on the horizon I'd ever seen in person that edged ever closer, did I have any privacy to collect her and put her plan in place. We fucked like frenzied bunnies for the last day, our bodies barely breaking contact until I slunk back across the island under cover of the darkness that blanketed the small stretch of land beneath a moonless night, already missing her touch to my skin and the feel of her wrapped in my arms.

What I wouldn't give to fall asleep with her.

Actual sleep.

But that wasn't to be, apparently. At least, not any time soon.

"Move. *Move.*" Commander – whatever his name was– snapped Jordie, gesturing at him with his gun.

The ship's pilot-cum-paleontologist cast me a sideways glance that morphed into a frown, jerking his head sideways. "The fuck is going on?"

I shrugged. "No idea." I didn't know what was going on, not when I got on the boat with them. "Just trying to do my job. I... left some of my kit up on the hill." I forced a smile. "I need to go and get it."

I'll come with you. "Jordie looked relieved to have a reason to avoid the maniac waving his gun about like it was a conductor's stick.

Everything was wrong. My gut curdled, and I shook my head quickly.

"Call of nature. Bad beans last night. Trust me. You don't wanna be here for this one, man."

Jordie grimace. "Done."

I powered on alone, heading for the entrance to

the caves, and hoped Blaze knew I was coming. Her hand spiking up out of the ground like a fiery fucking zombie emerging from beyond death's fold nearly did as I promised to Jordie.

"Fuck me, Sun Star." I helped her out of the crevices between the rocks, barely taking in her half flame form as she took on her usual body. If we got off the island together, I would have all the time in the world to explore her. I cast a glance over my shoulder. "They could see you here."

The stumpy shrubbery didn't cover much, including a naked glowing girl holding what looked like an ancient funeral urn. At least, that's what the little prison–how I knew she'd see it as once she was inside–looked like to me.

"Brought it!" She beamed up at me, her voice way too loud and glowy, a bit like her. Any other day I wanted her to be as loud as she could be but for now...

"Ssshh!" I hissed in her face, grabbing her arm and tugging her back to ground level.

The bush barely concealed her glowy companion lizard. My hiding spots officially sucked.

"That's not nice, Sinny Sinclair." Her hands were on her hips as she pushed back up to standing.

I yanked her down again as voices rose from the direction of the beach. "Fuckity fuck."

"That's cute."

"Hush." I covered her mouth with my hand, pulling her into me. She toppled half off balance against my chest. The jar trembled in her grip and tumbled toward the rocky surface she appeared from, zombie style.

I grabbed for it, getting a finger to its surface, and closed my hand around it seconds before it high fived the ground and broke into a dozen fragments or more, knowing the approximate age of it.

"You have to get in. Now," I hissed, popping the top.

A sweet aroma of something like honeysuckle and sunshine wafted out.

"Now?" She stared at me and the jar then back again with wide eyes. "You can't be serious. I'm not ready. We–we aren't ready." She reached into the fissure and Nahi jumped on the back of her hand. The tiny gecko ran the length of her arm and curled her around the crook of her elbow like a warrior's torc.

"Too late for *what ifs*, Sun Star." I removed my hand from her mouth and stroked her cheek. "It's now, or not at all. The boat's leaving and I don't think we're coming back."

I knew we weren't coming back. Whatever bee was under the military's bonnet told me they found what they were looking for and that boded really fucking badly for her, assuming my theory was sound.

She stared at me, the whites of her eyes showing as I proffered the jar with the heaviest heart.

This isn't how I meant to take you off the island.

I know.

Our silent conversation was broken by a flurry of heavy footsteps and a sharp bark of a voice I knew too well and hated in that moment.

"What's going on here?" Duncan stepped around my shrubbery, his eyes bugging from his face.

He wasn't alone. Behind him stood one of the armed military men–not the one who waved a gun like a flag on race day, though perhaps that wasn't a good thing. The hard look on this man's face was nothing short of evil.

I rose alone, trying to keep the shock off my face as I pressed the cork top into the clay jar with its ruined markings and nodded to Duncan.

"Just making sure we didn't leave without a few things I found late last night."

Fuck me if the glare he threw me didn't call me out on every damn inch of my bullshit statement.

But Blaze was safe in my hands. At least, I thought she was because just before I pressed the cork top into her jar, the bottom glowed. Not usual behavior for a jar, but this place made me reassess every single part of my previous belief system, even the parts I hadn't taken full stock of yet, and all because of her in the best ways.

Now all I had to do was get that cache of her trophies, all the things she collected during her long existence, and get those off the island, too.

With a military escort and no paper trail of anything I found in existence, that one was going to require the best explanation in the world, and right now I didn't have shit.

Duncan just stood still beside me as I straightened and looked him in the eye.

Then he smiled.

CHAPTER EIGHT

BLAZE

"Go with him."

Those were the last words I heard spoken about Sinclair for a long time. Then my jar was moving, jolting and swaying with the gait of a man I was unfamiliar with.

"Sinclair," I whispered only loud enough for Nahi to hear.

My lizard swirled around and through my flames like I wasn't really there at all. In this ethereal form, my body wasn't there any more than the flames of my hair held to a singular form. But for now, it was all I had to resort to in order to fit in the jar Sinclair carried.

Whoever carried it now.

Men's voices paired with waves lapping gently at the shoreline. Though there were no breakers, the sound was distinguishable from any other amidst the growing chatter for its cadence alone. But the longer I waited for a gentle tap of his fingers, a hushed, reassuring whisper in my direction, the more convinced I became that I was utterly alone. And trapped in this place, away from fresh air, I couldn't break back into my human form.

I was stuck.

And not near Sinclair.

Go with him.

Those words echoed through my flames. What, for a pee on a bush? Did my scientist geek need help with the most basic of functions now? I doubted that's what it was but when my jar thumped onto something hard, and a hand jammed my cork top down significantly, reducing my space, I barely held back the scream building within me.

My space shrank around me. Nahi's tiny feet frantically wiggled on the inside of the jar, and *through* me didn't help.

"I need air," I whispered as mine reduced.

Nahi stopped his frantic padding and curled on the bottom of the jar, staring pensively at me. Even his flames decreased a little. I sank down near him, and waited for the end I knew was coming.

When my current prison was swapped out for a glass one.

When the poking and prodding began.

If fire could cry, I would. Instead, my heart broke a thousand times over for believing a sexy man with no heart or belief that creatures like me would ever be seen as more.

Would ever be able to love, or be given love.

He abandoned me.

Perhaps it was his plan all along.

Nahi rubbed his head against my flames.

"I'm sorry," I whispered to him, testing the jar and knowing it wouldn't break in this weakened, faint form.

"...on board the ship. Less than useless." One of the voices I heard before Sinclair drifted away like so much deadwood broke me out of my reverie. How much more had I missed during my personal sob session?

He brought me books. He kissed my feet.

As if it meant nothing.

I strained at the edges of the cork, not caring that it smoked. Not caring that the sides of the damaged simple mud slab jar would soon be too hot to touch.

If I managed to bust out and ran, slinking into the cracks, maybe I could escape.

So many maybes, and they were all fallacy. I knew that as much as I knew getting Nahi to safety was a false hope, too. By emerging from the cave and falling in love, I walked straight into the trap the scientists and military with their bombs and test tubes and machines set for me long before.

I went willingly, because of a man who came bearing gifts.

"I should have stayed, waited for a warrior like back in the old times."

Nahi chittered his agreement softly, the sound too loud in my enclosed space.

More voices joined the first, angry ones.

"...the boat."

"–can't leave, that doesn't belong to–"

"Had a job to–"

"You can't take her!" That last nearly broke the jar as it tipped over and I recognized the voice. A breath of fresh air hit my flames, threatening them, but I was listening too hard to care.

Sinclair.

Maybe maybe maybe–

"This isn't your choice." The older, ball-like scientist, perhaps?

I strained for the next voice, dulling my glow to use my other senses.

"She isn't a toy, or a creature. She has a name, for fuck's sake!" Sinclair again, his agitation clear.

He came for me.

He loves me.

Okay, so that last part might be more than I should reasonably expect. But a girl could hope. A girl with a heart of fire and a wish for a not-Viking man because Sinny Sinclair would do just fine.

"Step aside, sir."

"I told you she stays."

"You need to step back. I won't ask again."

"I won't leave her."

"Sir, this is your final warning."

"For god's sake, Sinclair, step back. It's not like she's human."

"You—"

I never got to hear what Sinclair thought, because the gun's report only just covered the unearthly scream I released through a very human throat.

My world shattered. Clay shards flew in every direction. Sand kicked up as a body fell away from me. My feet were coated with a sticky substance, not related to the honeyed remnants of the perfume that the bottle once held.

The island's usually clean air stank of fear and death.

Sinclair.

His name ripped from my throat as I found him, lying prostrate on the sand that stained around him in a dark halo.

"No," I murmured through a raw throat. "*No.*" This single word was far from adequate for what I saw.

Hands locked at my elbows, towing me across the sand, away from him.

"You can't take her!" one of the other members of Sinclair's scientist crew shouted.

"Sir! Get back!"

"That's not right!"

"Stand still!"

Strained voices mixed with military orders that were flung around like so many pieces of shrapnel, the sort that bombarded my island for years in an effort to destroy what they could not control or contain.

"You never learn." The world stopped for me, because a world without Sinclair simply...faded.

Heat built in my chest. My eyes glazed and I didn't bother to look at the men hauling me away toward the smaller boat and the larger ship beyond. Or the two men with their hands over their mouths staring at Sinclair laid out on the sand, his mortality leached into my sands.

The water lapped nearer and once my feet touched it, I'd be immobile.

Unable to defend my island, Nahi, myself.

Unable to save him, if there was any saving to be had.

"No. No, no, no." I shook my head, my arms straining. I closed my eyes, already too on edge from my short incarceration. Already burning with revenge and the desire to keep on burning.

Everything.

Forever.

And so I did.

Energy remains the same. It just...changes.

The words inked on Sinclair's skin rang true, even if I paraphrased it a bit.

A mass of heat exploded from me, sweeping out in every direction. Those holding me disappeared in an instant, their existence wiped from the sand. The men near Sinclair dove for the ground, the grains above them glistening as they turned to glass in an instant. My world swayed and changed, flickering bright oranges and yellows, the color of the sunset predicting a perfect day.

Or a perfect storm.

"I loved you," I whispered to nothing and no one, none left to hear me.

The waves lapped at my feet, cooling, then freezing me. My heat plummeted, leaving me a shivering, shuddering mess. I might look human but inside I knew I could never fully pass for one. Maybe it was better this way.

The water's deathly touch that I avoided all these years, such a simple thing, was welcome now. I dropped to my knees, uncaring of the waves pooling around the blackened glass beneath me, or how far the radius extended.

How cold the water was, leeching inside me, and freezing my heart that tried to beat, but couldn't.

But it didn't matter, because I no longer cared. None of it mattered, nothing at all.

I sank into the hollow I created with my wrath, the dark passion of an island goddess displeased with the peoples who invaded her space.

Because the only one I wanted was gone.

Just like everyone else.

I never said I was nice.

I closed my eyes and let the water lap over my face, stealing my breath until it, too, stilled.

The water could have me.

CHAPTER NINE

SINCLAIR

I held her body in my arms, a breath away from begging a god–any god–to bring her back to me. The water swayed the larger ship beneath my feet. It had come in closer after her rage ripped the beach apart. My eyes were open enough at the time to witness her fury, and it was stunning.

Because of me.

Because she thought I was dead. And because they took her.

Still because of me.

The moment her body hit that water she froze. Literally a statue in place. It took all three of us remaining, me Jordie and Sam, to pull her free and urge her blue-tinged skin back to a pale white.

And because she was out, had extinguished the fire that kept her going for now, she appeared human. That's exactly what the soldiers saw who helped us pull her aboard their large ship with their medical bay where we currently sat.

A simple human, another scientist who survived the blast when others died.

I didn't care a whit about their losses, only her. Heartless? Immoral? None of that mattered.

Blaze breathed slowly in my arms, but showed no sign of waking. She hadn't in the five hours I held her while someone bandaged the gunshot wound to my shoulder that knocked me on my ass on the beach.

Blaze sorted that little problem out too by the simple expedient of blowing away every soldier on the beach, and Duncan, the backstabbing little mongrel.

Only Jordie and his husband were left, and me.

And her.

The moment I rose with the jar in my hand, Duncan had me and he knew it. I was a shitty liar at the best of times, always seeking truths, not avoiding them. This time I had more truths about the people I worked with and for, who, on occasion I might have called friend than I ever wanted.

Because I got to see what greed and the craving for treasure did to my little work family. Jordie helped me smuggle Nahi aboard too, not a single question asked about the thing that tried to flambé him every time he touched it.

But we got the gecko to the medical bay where it currently ran around a small Japanese stone garden where it couldn't set anything alight, chasing its tail. Jordie disappeared shortly after we settled, and I hadn't seen him since.

Blaze hadn't woken, stirred, or said a word. The soldiers believed our story that something buried in the sand must have exploded, as we were all warned before we set foot back on the island for our second trip.

And because there was no one to contradict our story, and we were well away from the site, there were no unfortunate questions asked, either. I earned a few sideways glances for my gunshot wound, but that a gun might have gone off during the blast wasn't out of the question. I was ruled out as a simple collateral mishap.

For now, I had been assigned a room I hadn't seen, and rocked Blaze in my arms, whispering nonsense things to her.

Jordie's head popped into the room. "Come with

me right now,' he hissed, gesturing frantically. "And grab your damn lizard."

"She hasn't woken." I frowned at him, gesturing down at Blaze.

"No and she bloody well won't, not here and not safely, unless you come with me right now." Jordie's voice lowered to a hiss.

I stared at him. "What have you done?"

"Found you a way out."

I followed him, the lizard smoking slightly inside my sleeve, as I carried Blaze off the boat and into the craft one we arrived in, nodding to the soldiers who waved us off as Jordie powered the thing across the water in record time.

"That was...uneventful?" Jordie's husband, Sam, greeted me with a smile and a can of cold soda. "The *Mishap* wasn't half as damaged as we all expected. A little sullied by the military, but we can deal with that. They want to get back to whatever the hell they do, cover up their next mess, and we are free to bring ourselves home, seeing as we have a pilot who can get us back there."

"I forgot you were a ship's pilot." I turned to Jordie. "You wear many hats. I'm grateful." More than I could say. They still asked no questions as I stared down at Blaze. "You must...want to know things."

"Yes," said Sam.

"No," said Jordie.

I laughed. "She lived there. It's what–who–they were keeping in. I don't think their mission was well known. Just another regular check up on old bombs and what not." I shrugged.

"Did you know she could...?" Sam puffed out his cheeks and expanded his hands in a simulation of an explosion.

"I've only known her for three days, but it feels like a decade," I whispered, pulling Blaze tighter to my chest.

"Sometimes you know." Jordie wrapped his arm around Sam's shoulder and pulled him in close. The warmth and love emanating between them left my heart aching.

I brushed hair back from her face, willing the strands to glow but there wasn't so much as a spark left in her. Was this how she spent her eternity, sleeping away eons in response to each outburst? I wasn't sure if it was her explosion of heat that left her unconscious, but the way she turned blue the moment the water touched her skin had been terrifying.

Her lizard slithered out of my smoking shirt and jumped onto her chest, turning circles and nesting there.

"Cute," I murmured, stroking his back, too.

His blue flames intensified, warming the cabin to a decent temperature.

Jordie stripped off his jacket. "Alright. Let's get this boat the fuck away from this place."

I watched Blaze for a moment longer and shook my head. "No. There's something else we need to do first."

By sunrise the next morning, Blaze still hadn't woken. Sea water sloshed against the hull of the much smaller boat than the ship we escaped, and the military absence was significant in the easy silence that pervaded our return to civilization.

Jordie sat in the pilot's chair, studying the horizon and cuddling a cold mug of tea.

"Thank you for doing this." My voice came out slightly rusty with disuse.

I barely spoke the day before, holding Blaze to me while her gecko slept on her chest. That seemed to warm her, and a glow returned to her skin.

For a few scant hours, I had hope.

Then the sun dipped below the horizon, and her glow faded, as though she retreated from the world.

"Maybe we should take her back." Jordie didn't look at me, still studying the sky's pale yellow streaks that reflected in the water. "Did you think of that?"

I swallowed hard. "Yeah." *But I don't want to.*

"She killed on that beach."

"They invaded her island. Her home. She thought–"

She thought they killed me. I saw the terror written across her face in stark relief as the sun hit her glowing skin. The way her eyes widened, the feral sound that tore from her throat as she looked at me where I lay too stunned to respond.

Then it was over, and she curled in a pool of water, in a crater of black glass six feet in diameter, drowning in her sorrow.

For the first time in who knew how long, I wanted to be selfish. I wanted to keep her.

She's not a toy.

No, she's mine.

My inner battle went unheard by Jordie who scowled at the horizon like it personally insulted him. I searched around for an icebreaker.

"How did you go from being the captain of a boat

to becoming a paleontologist?" That was the first thing that fell out of my mouth.

Jordie finally turned to face me, amusement curling his lips. "I'm also a Justice of the Peace. You can be more than just a scientist, you know, Sinclair. The world does turn on its axis while you're not studying geothermal rocks. Get a hobby. Hell, get five. Or a dog."

"Yeah, but the world might blow up at any time." I shrugged, ignoring that last pointed barb.

Forget her.

But I couldn't.

I mean, he was right about the dog. Maybe I could borrow Nahi for a while...

"You are a doomsdayer."

"And you're a hoarder." Sam wrapped his arms around Jordie's neck and kissed his cheek.

I looked away, wanting to offer them privacy seeing as it was my fault we were in this mess to start. The other half of me couldn't stand seeing people so in love when my own heart died in that black glass crater on the sand of an island we left behind a day ago.

My chest ached at the memory, but I ignored that, too. We were several days out of the nearest outpost, or so Jordie assured me when we took the *Mishap* and ran.

The military thankfully were as glad to see the end of us as we were of them, having their own issues with dealing with the death of a small cohort due to someone's theoretical ineptitude, believing my lie about her being my last minute intern.

Or the island goddess who lost her temper.

She killed.

Jordie's words haunted me as I turned around to find myself face to glowing hair threads. A pair of magenta eyes burned up at me, her expression dangerous and filled with the sort of uncontained fury that could do exactly what I said to our pilot moments ago and destroy the world.

I loved her all the more for it.

"You were dead," she accused me in the low voice I associated with a campfire about to burst into full flame. "I saw you. On the sand, Sinclair."

No Sinny. No fun little barbs or jibes.

"I'm okay. It was a shoulder shot." I pressed my hand to my shoulder where it was bandaged beneath my shirt. "Seeing you fall into that water and not get up...that hurt a whole lot more."

"You're up." Sam bounced on his toes near us, dancing while Jordie shushed him gently.

"Do you want to eat? A drink?" Jordie offered, gently disengaging his husband where he clung to my elbow, practically glowing with happiness.

Between Blaze and I, none of that happened.

Between us sat a void I wasn't sure how to cross.

She swallowed, her chin hiking high though her blazing eyes that matched her name and never left mine. "I thought I would be alone again, Sinclair. Alone and put in a bottle and chopped up–"

"Like a stew?" Sam glanced between us.

"Yeah, like a stew." The corner of my mouth lifted. "That's a scary thought, being boiled alive in a pot as a fire goddess who can control the temperatures around her."

Her eyes narrowed to slits. I swore she was about to start spitting brimstone at me. For her, I'd wear that. Let her destroy me. Not fight her. Because I loved her that much.

Her mouth dropped open. "You do?"

I closed mine with a snap. *Shit.*

Blaze huffed in my direction. "Captain." She swiveled slowly on her heel, breaking our eye contact for the first time. "You *are* a captain, aren't you?"

Jordie cleared his throat. "Yes, Ma'am."

"And you have all the rights of the old ways?"

It took him a second to interpret that, but a slow smile spread over his face. "Yes, ma'am. I do."

Blaze nodded decisively. "Then let's get to it."

She grabbed my elbow and hauled me toward the bow.

"What are we doing?" I tried to put on the brakes, but my girl was strong after her nap, and it was all sorts of sexy. "Blaze?" I managed, whetting my lips.

She spun in a tight circle to face me, gently cupping my shoulder, the heat of her palm warming my wound.

"We're getting married."

CHAPTER TEN

BLAZE

I wore a white terry toweling bathrobe that belonged to someone else, and carried a coffee mug filled with colored pencils delicately wrapped in one of the old grass skirts I pulled from my trunk. Bless Sinny-Sinclair for thinking of it and risking limbs and his general existence for going back to get my collection. Nahi curled in the bottom of the mug and smoked the pencils a bit, but I figured we would get through the ceremony without too many incidents.

After all, two fire creatures on a boat in the middle of a sea that would mean an end to my own life and Nahi's with no land in sight probably wasn't the best option, but it was the one we had to work with.

Sinclair stood by my side in front of Jordie, his hand wrapped around my waist. He wore a fresh black military tee shirt that had been left behind in their exodus. His ripped jeans looked somewhat worse for wear, though he combed his hair back from his face, all dapper like. I'd read a prohibition gargoyle romance while he took his time perfecting himself, even though there was no need.

My hair curled around both of us, and when he looked at me with sparkling eyes, hooded in a way that left my lips tingling, my lizard wasn't the only thing smoking.

"Rein it in, just for a few more days until you're on land and off my boat, pretty please," Jordie murmured in a low voice. "Shall we get started?"

I nodded, barely able to take my eyes off Sinclair. Nor did I manage to listen to the words our stand in celebrant said. I'd had enough proposals and warriors claiming to bring me to this exact situation in my eons to know the general gist. Time or apart, the idea was the same. We merged souls, loved until life extinguished, and carried on after. Or something like that. My interpretation might be slightly different to everyone else's, but Sinclair didn't seem to mind.

"Blaze?" Jordie looked at me expectantly.

I blinked and watched Sinclair mouth the words I needed to say.

"I do," I said promptly.

Jordie grinned and I zoned out again, studying Sinclair's dark eyes shot with the gold of a rising sun and smoldering like a volcano ready to pop. My happy little haze didn't break until he slid the little black squishy band he pulled from his pocket on that first day and rolled the O-ring over my finger. I sank back into him when he wrapped his arms around me and snogged me for all he was worth.

And I snogged him back just as fiercely. My Sinclair. My Sinny-Sin.

"I love you," he murmured into my hair, then pulled my mouth back to his, ignoring Jordie's protests of *enough*, though a soft round of applause broke out around us.

And in the bottom of my coffee mug, my salamander smoked happily.

EPILOGUE

SINCLAIR

I watched Blaze sort through my collection of retro computer games. Nintendo seemed to be her favorite, so she couldn't wrap the concept of the various genres. Still, we would get there. The other consoles she discarded, claiming they were too real, and I knew she hated first person shooter games. Not that I blamed her, after our experiences with guns together.

But blaze displayed her happiness in plenty of other ways while Nahi toasted my kitchen bench with his fiery butt. She had a love of all things anime, which made my little heart ridiculously happy.

"This one?" I pointed at a Smurfs game, but she

shook her head and shivered, wrapping her arms around herself.

Blaze stared hard at a couple of the fantasy games, and carefully slid them aside. I shook my head, sliding down the back of the sofa to curl my body around her on the rug. When I wrapped my hands around her waist to pull her back into me, her hair's flames caressed my cheeks, but they didn't burn me anymore. Not even the slightest amount. Being on the beach on her island that day...it changed us.

Or maybe her flames were testing me. Perhaps they just liked me now. Either way, impromptu cuddling was certainly a whole lot easier than the fear that consumed us both in the past.

"This one?" I studied the faded label of the game she held up, its split corners curled and slightly yellowed. I didn't quite recognize it, but I remembered it had a fair bit of violence she wouldn't like.

"Maybe not," she murmured. "What about..." She trailed off, her hands darting about, unable to choose from the pile.

It wasn't a problem she seemed to have with books, but that was okay.

I caught her fluttering hands and squeezed her fingers, finally finding the courage to broach what I needed to with her, but had been holding back, fear my old friend raising its ugly fucking head. "You know you can go back to the island whenever you like. "

"What?" She twisted where she sat, staring at me. I brushed hair back across her cheek until she made the happy sounds I loved from her most. "What if they start bombing again? What if someone finds me?"

"The island has memories for you," I said slowly. "We have money. Maybe..."

Kahoolawe had been her home for so long, and we both knew she wasn't fitting into modern life easily. She tried, but there was so much white noise and chatter in daily life that like with the games, choices became too hard and frustrating for her.

"I know, sexy Sinclair boy. But that doesn't make you rich. You're not a tribe chief."

I shook my head. "I'm not chief, but you are a goddess, and you have a collection of one-thousand-year-old mementos sitting in a box under my bed."

She watched me curiously over her shoulder, her pink eyes lighting with their usual flame in the sexiest way possible. "You found that, huh?"

I smiled fondly, running my fingers along her jawline and kissed the tip of her nose. "Yeah. I found those. And I did a little research, too." She said nothing, just stared at me, though her body heated up a few extra degrees in all the best ways. "I know the grass skirts and headdresses are part of the island's history. And that gives the owner a few extra dimes of leverage."

"What's a dime?" She frowned at my terminology.

"We can do money another day, fire girl. Stay with me. What might be possible is that the island is under a government style protection. While they can't sell it exactly, the owner of the historical pieces gets a sort of claim, and the land can be leased to a trust."

"What's a trust?" Her head rested on my shoulder. "You're talking Glooobedebooks to me."

"Gobbledygook. But that was super cute. A trust means you and your family can..." I thought about it for a minute and went for simplicity even if the terms weren't overly perfect in translation. "It means you can go back without fear of people pushing you off the island."

"I can?" She blinked at me, her lips pursing, and I swore smoke rose from her hair. "For...when? For... how long?"

"Two hundred years."

"Two hundred years." She mouthed the words, though no sound emanated from her.

"Yep." I grinned at her proudly. "I have paperwork and we can read it over a thousand times until you understand it all. And....I might have put a little caveat in there that says something about potential claims and future ownership for your children."

She swallowed hard. "You know I'll live longer than two hundred years."

"I know that."

"And that our children will outlive you, and maybe be...like me. If I can have any."

"I get that too." I booped her nose because she was so damn cute.

"And–"

"And we can start right now." I rolled us onto the rug, pressing my body weight over hers.

She let me kiss her until our bodies were grinding urgently together, then shifted, her heels hooked behind my thighs. Suddenly she perched on my hips, undulating gently over me. The strings holding her top together–she wasn't a fan of constricting clothes or spaces–unraveled like they had a mind of their own. The scrap of material fell away, baring her breasts to me.

I sucked in a long breath, rising up to catch their

perfect weight in my hands, but she knocked me away, her eyes glowing–really actually glowing–with this magenta fire that existed within only her.

My goddess.

"No touching. But keep going," she said differently, except for those eyes that damned my soul to an eternity of servitude to her.

I was good with that.

"Going...like this?" I rocked with her, enjoying the way her breath hitched maybe a tad too much.

"Keep talking," she murmured faintly, dropping her hands forward to knead my chest with short nails. "Just don't stop." Her fingers slipped between us, and she struggled to free my cock, bunching her skirt around her thighs with her other hand.

"You look like something wild and untamed." I tried not to gasp when her hand curled around me, squeezing tight. "So beautiful."

She huffed. "Flattery will get you everywhere."

I smiled, though I had to grit my teeth to manage without letting out another groan. "The older tribes claimed they used your island for celestial navigation, and specific rights but it was you they were orbiting and worshiping, wasn't it?" I trailed my fingertips along her bare thighs where her skirt pulled over her hips, exposing herself to me. "It was you they navigated around. My Sun Star."

She rose fluidly over me, dropping her hips and impaling herself on my hard length.

A groan ripped free from my throat. I swore I'd never get used to that feeling, not even if I buried myself inside her heat every damn day. Several times, if I had my way. But this girl...she held the reins, and she knew it.

I wouldn't have her any other way than what came most naturally to her. Not when she'd been shoved about by warriors past. A goddess got to have her own way at some point, right?

Blaze rose and fell over me, her hands drifting down to clasp mine as she rode me to the fiery pits of some mystical dimension and back. All I could see was her eyes, and the heart she laid out before me alongside mine.

Her body shuddered with its first climax. I pressed out linked hands to her hips, urging her rolling gait harder. Deeper. Pushing my hips up from the floor, I watched her face for any sign she liked what I did, trying to read her, learn her. Blaze's head tipped back, her lips parting in a silent scream that ripped through me nonetheless.

I railed her, gritting my teeth until pleasure

ripped down my spine. Swearing softly, I mimicked her stance, my head pushing back into the rug, spearing my hips deep into her. My roar filled the room where her pleasure rippled silently around us, and we crashed together in a tangle of sweat and limbs, and the sort of afterglow that remained for the rest of the day.

Maybe longer.

"So, what were we playing?" She mumbled softly against my chest minutes later while her hair and I warred for dominance in worshiping those perfect shoulders.

"Whatever you want, Sun Star." I kissed the top of her head and helped her fix her top, though I had no issue with her not wearing clothes, even if others might object. Who was I to deny a ten thousand year old fire goddess who chose a mere mortal, after all?

"The island sounds good," she said carefully.

I tipped her head back to find her brows knitted. "You're thinking."

"No shit." She grinned at my comical expression. "And swearing is fun."

"There are some good words." I stretched my calves, rearranging us with my back to the sofa's legs and her in my lap. "So...what's on that pretty mind?"

She reached across me, all slithery and limber

and so goddamn *hot* in all the ways that matter and a few that probably didn't. None of that mattered. I loved every aspect of her.

"Mario Kart?" She stared at me owlishly, tapping her finger on the island track pictured at the top corner of the case.

I grinned. "You know that one is four player? That means we can have a party."

"A what?" she frowned. "Does that mean we still get to play?"

"With friends." I nodded soberly while her stunning face lit up.

"With Marcus and Jordie?"

I grinned. They'd been her regular teachers in the way the world worked now while she shared everything she knew with the pair of paleontologists to their utter, geeky bliss.

"The same."

"I'm all in." She wiggled, proud of nailing the expression.

I grinned and cupped her cheeks, pressing my lips to her hers.

"Me too, Sun Star."

Loved Blaze's book?
Please leave a REVIEW.

Read on for the first chapter of
KRAKEN'S VOW.

SNEAKY PEEK AT KRAKEN'S VOW

LANI

Numbers ran through my head in the opposite direction they ran across the screen, each making less sense than the next. Tapping at the keyboard in a distinct lackluster style, I glanced down at the next row of stats, or tried to. The whole lot blurred and no amount of blinking dry eyes could make sense of a single digit.

"Gah," I croaked, my throat as dry as my eyeballs for all the sound it elicited in true personal style.

"I can't understand you, Lauren."

"Lani." I corrected the auto AI response that kept me company in the middle of a conjunction of three Alaskan fjords met, the lip of the sea just beyond. Four years in my icebox of a lab, and the silly bitch still didn't know my name. "It's Lani, Usan." My petty comeback fell flat because my snarky AI didn't come preprogrammed with a sense of humor.

"Could you repeat that?" Susan continued on as though I'd just spouted utter rubbish and ignored it.

Perhaps I had.

It could be the function of sitting alone day in and out trying to work out the TOG or thermal resistance of a fabric against its hydrostatic head to create a researcher's suit that meant more time under water. More research, less issues after a lot of dives. Deeper dives...that last I particularly struggled with. I'd chosen the Alaskan Fjords because it meant medium conditions to test in, though my results were fast fading.

The other reason was that hardly anyone bothered me. Isolation was assured, and that suited me just fine.

Frowning, I ignored Susan's emotional ineptitude and concentrated on my data. Within minutes the numerals resembled cuneiform. Cold dregs and sloppy grains tickled my throat as I shut down.

"What time is it?" I asked the lab at large.

"It is six a.m."

I blinked. That meant I'd gone another night without sleep. *Shit.* "Creating a lab without windows wasn't a smart move." Though it had seemed clever at the time. No distractions.

"You don't need visual cues to operate," Susan reminded me.

"No, *you* don't need sunrises and sunsets to reset your internal clock. Humans do," I grumbled, swiping a hand over my face. "I'm going topside."

"You are in need of several items for the dry room."

Double shit. Supplies meant heading into town and peopling. I wasn't prepared to face that just yet. Topside, however, was synonymous with fresh air. That I could handle. Nothing like a stunning-albeit frigid-Alaskan morning to bring out the happy mind drugs. Bonus of heading into the village meant more coffee beans. At least, that's what I told myself as I climbed the three flights of steep, diamond plate metal stairs.

My thighs and calves trembled by the third flight. How long had I been in that chair? My ass hadn't gone numb, which was always a nice surprise. That and the fact it hadn't gone flat, like a wombat.

I climbed the small ladder and spun the door wheel on the waterproofed hatch, bracing myself for the blast of icy wind to assail my face, followed by the shaft of glorious sunlight bouncing off the surrounding glaciers at this time of year. The wheel jerked, my hands slipping on its hard, cold surface. I pushed up with every ounce of strength, wondering against the feasibility of the design. The waterproof factor protected my lab from weather of all sorts, which meant little maintenance. If the structure toppled from its stem buried deep in the near-center of the fjord into a watery grave, I'd disappear beneath the white caps that brushed the sides of my lab and disappear into nothingness, existing until my air ran out.

Not that it was likely to happen, and always the scientist, I was a stats girl through and through. Risk and longevity were a set of numbers calculated to constantly stream through my head.

The hatch whooshed open under my determination, and bright white light filtered into my lab. I pulled myself out, perched on the edge and took in my surroundings. Glaciers and forest land surrounded me. The fjord sliced through the middle of the spectacular iced peaks that retreated year by year.

I took my solace in the silence while I could still appreciate their beauty.

At the far end of the blue and white framed valley, a small fishing village-town was too big a word for the remote, scattered populace-sat with just enough resources to allow me to stock up without traveling too far from the ocean, my lab or into the interior.

My old walkaround tapped the side rail that ran around the edge of my lab's hard exoskeleton in a gentle rhythm. Wind blustered around my circulator lab, the water tugging between white caps and the pull of the tide in the narrow fjord. The building protruded above the water's surface with just enough circular walkways for me to make my way to the boat and deal with technical crap if anything broke in rough weather. Which was hopefully never.

I sucked in a last breath of air that froze my lungs for an instant before my body thawed beneath the pure intake. Shimmying back into the lab, I ignored Susan's attempts to keep me working and headed for my room. A quick change from leggings and geeky tee that said *bananas are radioactive,* the letters circled around a glowing specimen of the elongated fruit left me more socially acceptable. The local hamlet understood my sense of humor about as well as Susan did.

Jeans, thermals and a fluffy jacket that had the world's best snuggle factor ever and boots signified my civvies' attire. I climbed back up the stairs, checking my steps for the day. *Seven hundred.*

"Send the list to my phone please," I said absently into my phone, running my head through everything we needed, even though I knew she'd send me a reminder before I hit the village anyway.

"Enjoy your trip, Lisa," Susan cooed.

"Enjoy your solitude. Auto settings Suzie Q."

"I don't know what you mean," overran Susan's platonic response, "Automated conditions activated."

I closed my eyes and prayed my AI wasn't developing a split personality.

Spray feathered the curved windscreen in tiny droplets as I pushed my walkaround the length of the fjord. The old boat I'd bought from a local family when I arrived didn't go fast, but it was certainly better than kayaking the miles to the village. Plus, it had weather cover and space for supplies which meant less trips.

The glacier's beauty still awed me, even after years of living in the area. Their pale blue glow alight with the morning that filtered light along the water and its surrounds, they were the perfect setting for an Ice Queen fairytale.

Pity I have zero allegiance with neither ice, nor royalty.

I grinned at the thought, snuggling deeper into my fluffy coat. Waterproof on the outside, warmth on the inside. I might be a stats girl but that didn't mean I couldn't appreciate comfort...especially in the wake of zero human contact for the majority of my year.

"One hour, get everything, go home." *Right, Susan?* I didn't say the last part out loud, though if I slipped up and started talking to the AI who didn't exist in the clunker of the boat I drove, it wouldn't be the first time.

Home. I closed my eyes for a minute, knowing there was no other water traffic, and my steering wasn't that shit. It had been a long damn time since I went home, though I doubted there would be much there to recognize now. Or maybe there would, and the world turned on without my presence instead.

The tiny village of Hythe-that literally meant landing place of boats, very original-had been welcoming, for the most part. There might be gossip when I wasn't around, but the pure speculation on my part was based in fact. The town was filled with the loveliest people who also managed to keep their reputations as horrendous gossips. The sweetest anglers were the worst of the lot.

I might not call any place *home* right now, but the locals likely traded stories the moment I hopped back on my boat and headed back to my lab.

My sterile, personless lab, where I talked to an AI who couldn't remember my name instead of real people.

What a humbling thought.

I gripped the steering wheel that warmed beneath my hands, cracking my eyes open in time to see the horizon tilt sideways, and a shower of spray slam down over the front of my lurching boat.

I flung an arm over my face to shield my eyes though the windscreen did that for me, leaving one hand on the wheel that spun crazily, wrenching my wrist past the point of no return. Something *popped* that should never have made the noise. Still working on automatic somewhere in my brain I wrenched the steering wheel back the way it should have been, leveling the boat.

A delayed pain response ripped a scream from my lips, white blanking out my vision for a second. A moment that stilled, my brain stalling at the event unfolding before my eyes. Silver flashed somewhere in my pain-blinded state, too fast for me to translate into reality. Elongated swells and curves of an apex predator paired with a man's dark head.

If angels were feathered godlings then this-this creature had crawled free from the abyss of hell.

All over-long body, all the wrong shape, a flicker of-*fuck me, is that a tentacle?*-and silver eyes, reflective as his skin that might have been made of metal.

What in all the seven hells am I seeing?

A scream that had nothing to do with the pain in my hand that dulled in the face of monstrous fear lodged between my throat and my mouth and refused to eject from my body. As though I knew that if I screamed, the sound would prove the scenario was real.

My strained mind interpreted the broken image as a giant shark thing leaping across the bow of the boat. Water cascaded over the guarded helm, dripping down the neck of my jacket.

And then....nothing.

The water swirled in eddies along the sides of the boat, tiny white caps drifting by as the waves settled back into their familiar rhythm.

I blinked, and might have hallucinated it all.

Do injuries create mirages?

Maybe I'd been staring at the water for too long. Maybe a torn tendon did that.

Tendons and tentacles. Was there something in that?

Maybe there were things in the water beneath my feet.

Bile rose in my throat, stalling in the same place as my scream had frozen before it dissipated, too. The whole situation left me with nothing more than an old boat rocking unsteadily on its haul in an incoming tide and a new shot of pain that injected my brain with adrenaline.

I clutched my wrist against my chest, gripping the wheel through that, mercifully, stayed still as my chest heaved. I stared into the water, searching for anything that looked like a weird ass eel or mini leviathan, but the waters calmed as my boat powered on.

Unwilling to stop the boat from moving and unable to prevent my body from trembling, I ferreted around for the first aid box stowed safely in one of the hatches. Thankfully, the contents remained protected by the stoic little cream plastic box. I extracted a twist hot/cold hiker's ice pack and as soon as the green sludgy contents of the pack came to life, I pressed it around my wrist that had already started to swell.

My head ran through the *R.I.C.E* theory-rest, ice, compression, elevate-while I convinced myself that the area had a weird large fish that chased a squid across my windscreen. But no matter what I told myself in the ten minutes between incident and dock, my mind refused to buy the fantasy I was selling.

Plus, don't forget the tentacles.

And that brought up images I couldn't forget. Once, horny as hell, I'd tried to sneak erotic lit past Susan's download checker. That had that been a massive fail that resulted in me staging an intervention between Susan and the internet, and having the birds and the bees talk with a computer on a bad hair day. I'd also corrupted my AI. We spent the next few hours discovering tentacle porn and enjoying the randomness factor far too much.

The memory lasted just long enough to distract me from the fading pain in my wrist. I snorted at my own stubbornness-one of the reasons I enjoyed my alone time so much. I didn't have to deal with objecting to other's opinions on my life goals...and they didn't get to influence my decisions on anything.

So, I was a control freak who lived in the middle of a frozen valley, in the middle of a fjord, with creepy ass fish. The snort became a giggle and the giggle subsided one hair shy of hysterics.

That helped with the shaking but not the *shaken* part. I scanned the water, checking behind me at intervals in true-blonde-in-the-boat horror movie style, but nothing jumped out at me all the way along the fjord to Hythe's small dock.

Read KRAKEN'S VOW

ABOUT THE AUTHOR

Raven Hush writes paranormal & BDSM romance and exists on a diet of red wine and coffee. When she isn't romancing the monster under her bed, she writes contemporary romance and suspense as *USA Today bestselling* author Sofia Aves and kidlit under a not-so-super-secret pen name. Raven has worked with Romance Writers of Australia as Marketing and Events Manager and at the Romance Cafe Publishing in their Marketing and PR department for four years. She is a stay-at-home mum living near Brisbane, Australia with her three crazies and two german shepherds who like to pose whilst wrestling. Raven writes in her own dragon bookish cave and wrangles her alpacas daily. One day, she might even write about them.

Bookishly stalk Raven:

WEBSITE

AMAZON

BOOKBUB

INSTAGRAM

TWITTER

FACEBOOK

Silent Sentinels Duet

Reflections of Silence

Echoes in the Void

Monsters In New York

Feral Moon Rising (2025)

Writing Romantasy as

SOFIA SHELLEY

Dead Poets Sorority

Writing Reverse Harem Dark Romance as

DOVE PRIEST

Recurve Ridge

Writing Steamy Romance as Sofia Aves

Blue Blooded Brothers

Collision

Politics & Paperwork

Blindsided

Sentinel

Mugshots & Candy Canes

Impact

Reckoning

Red Hart Ranch

Snow on the Range

Siren on the Range

Sundown on the Range

Spirit on the Range

Ash on the Range

Mistletoe on the Range

Forgotten Mountain Man

Gourd Enough To Eat

Texan Devils

Ranger's Wish

Ranger Bedevilled

Ranger's Passion

Ranger's Fury

Ranger's Wrath

Ranger's Storm

Snapdragons & Seductions

Summer with a Ranger

Merry with a Ranger

Playing to Win

Off Boarding

Vicious Slash

Zero Pointer

Off Stage Fling

Rippton Allstars

Crushing It

Glacial Force

Rippton Creatives

Study Games

Make Me, Break Me

Twisted Obsession

Spring Break with a Mafia Prince

A Royally Fake French Menage

Jericho Chimeras

Puck Me Always

Puck My Heart

Puck me Sideways

Z Boys

King

Joker

Hearts

Ace

Mayhem & Mistletoe

Ruski

Fast Track to Love

Speed Trap

Klauss Brothers

Zander

Keegan

Gallo Empire *with Jade Marshall*

Splintered Vows

Fractured Vows

Fierce Vows

Savage Covenant

Rom Coms

She's A Hot Christmas Mess

Boats, Moats and Root Beer Floats

Kidlit writing as

JO SEYSENER

The OCD Elf

Greg and the Egg

writing YA as

JOSS PHOENIX

Alchem Academy

Hide From Us